FINDING HOME

RICK WOOD

About the Author

Finding Home

Rick Wood is a British writer born in Cheltenham.

His love for writing came at an early age, as did his battle with mental health. After defeating his demons, he grew up and became a stand-up comedian, then a drama and English teacher, before giving it all up to become a full-time author.

He now lives in Loughborough, where he divides his time between watching horror, reading horror, and writing horror.

Also by Rick Wood

AFTER

Chapter One

Gus had tried making a roast dinner himself once. It had not gone well.

He'd bought most of the vegetables already sliced and frozen, and they tasted like tinned food you would only eat in the apocalypse. The potatoes were still hard, the peas were a strange consistency between mushy and not mushy, and the smash he'd mixed out the packet was still water and powder.

Yet when Janet did it, it looked like a professional chef had come in and taken over his house, filling it with a mixture of delectable aromas. The steamed parsnips were crispy on the outside and soft on the inside, the balls of stuffing had the right amount of fluff and the right amount of sage and the right amount of everything, and the carrots were steamed to perfection. The table was finished off with pigs in blankets, mashed potato with a hint of cheese, and Yorkshire puddings that tasted like they had only been mixed and heated minutes ago.

And then the final part, the piece de la resistance —chicken with the skin browned, just as he liked it, with steam rising and gravy sauce sizzling. Saliva filled Gus's mouth like a manic storm.

Janet placed the chicken before him.

"Would you carve, my dear?" she asked, leaning against him, pressing her hip against his cheek and *damn* how did she look so hot in that apron?

"That doesn't seem fair," Gus replied, unable to help himself grinning. "You cooked this wonderful meal. Surely you should cut the chicken?"

He did feel guilty. It didn't really matter, he knew – but it seemed wrong that, just because he was the husband, that he was one who was seen to do the most important part; when it was nothing compared to the effort his wife had gone to.

But she just bent over, kissed him delicately on the cheek, and whispered in his ear:

"I wouldn't dream of taking the pleasure away from you."

His body tingled. A wave of arousal swept over him and he couldn't help but watch her buttocks as they sauntered back to the kitchen.

"Come on, Daddy," came Lacey's delightful voice from beside him. "You always carve the chicken."

She beamed up at him, proud and doting, the vision of a perfect child. He couldn't be prouder of his daughter.

"Yeah, Gus," said Sadie in the next seat along. "It's your job."

He marvelled at the sight of Sadie.

For starters, he marvelled at how she was able to form such coherent sentences. Normally she was barely able to put a few words together, mostly speaking in syllables and grunts – yet, here she was, speaking perfectly.

What's more, she was dressed very differently. Her hair was no longer scraggly and stringy; the mosses and tufts had gone, and she was wearing a neat, flowery dress rather than the dirty rags she refused to change.

"I agree," said Donny. "You have to carve, Gus. It's tradition."

Donny.

Donny?

What was he doing here?

Thinking nothing of it, and not wanting to ruin the moment, he lifted the carving knife and started from the rear of the chicken, cutting it into slices.

"What's the matter?" asked Desert.

"What?" Gus responded, unsure.

"You look... I don't know. Perturbed."

"I just..." He looked to Donny again. "Wasn't expecting you all to be here."

"Why wouldn't we be here?" Whizzo asked. "You invited us, didn't you?"

Did he?

He couldn't remember.

Did he invite all of them?

It seemed a strange thing to do.

But he didn't want to argue and did not want to seem rude. Nothing to sully the moment. After all, Janet had cooked enough for everyone. It was only going to go to waste otherwise, wasn't it?

"I'm sorry Prospero couldn't be here," Donny said to Desert.

Desert smiled sweetly – although Gus could see there was something else behind that smile. It appeared endearing, but only Gus seemed to pick up on how it was almost... sadistic.

"Why are you sorry?" Desert asked.

"I almost feel like it was my fault," Donny responded.

"Your fault?" Her voice was rising. "Of course it's your fault! You ki–"

"We'll have none of that," Janet said, taking her seat at the table and raising her glass of wine. "A toast. What shall we toast to?"

Murmurs of suggestions floated around the table, ending when Lacey turned to her father.

"What do you want to toast to, Daddy?"

They all turned and looked to him, awaiting his verdict.

What were they going to toast to?

What could they toast to?

"Friends," Gus decided, raising his glass. "Old and new, and reunited."

Just as they all raised their glasses and began the first syllable of "friends," the front door opened and closed, and a man walked in. He closed his umbrella, put it in the corner, and rubbed his drenched hair.

Gus looked to this man peculiarly.

He knew him.

He knew the man very well.

But who was he?

"I'm ever so sorry I was late," the man said, his voice carrying a lot of wealth and a lot of education.

"It's okay," said Janet, standing up and putting an arm around him.

This made Gus livid. He wasn't sure why, he had never been the jealous type; yet his wife's arm around this man's back somehow made his fingers grip his napkin, unknowingly scrunching it up and tearing it into tufts.

"That's okay, Eugene," said Lacey, standing and rushing over to the man, putting her arms around him also. "We're just glad you could come. Did you bring your daughter as well?"

"Of course," Eugene replied, revealing a girl standing beside him. "I bought my Laney too."

Gus knew this girl.

He'd rescued this girl.

From London.

Rescued.

Driven out just as London was bombed.

But he also knew something else as well.

He knew that this was not Eugene's daughter.

She never had been.

"What's that?" Eugene asked with a pleasant smile.

"You're lying," Gus said, this time loud enough to be heard, but still with a falter.

"I'm what?" Eugene said, poised between being offended and laughing at a joke.

"That is not your daughter. She never was. You are full of shit."

"Gus, please!" Janet exclaimed.

"Yeah, come on, Gus," Donny said. "Don't make a scene."

"And you..." Gus said, glaring at Donny, not noticing his own arms beginning to shake. "You... You are working with him! You used to be my friend but you tried to kill me!"

"Gus–" Desert tried.

"And you killed Prospero!"

"Daddy!" Laney cried, covering her ears. "You're upsetting me!"

It was at this point Gus realised he was standing. He couldn't remember rising from his chair, but he somehow had. Everything felt so wrong.

His wife. She was dead.

His daughter. She was...

"What's happening?" Gus cried out.

"Gus, are you feeling okay?" Janet asked, advancing toward him.

"Who are you?" Gus growled, and Janet backed away – moving further toward Eugene, which only incensed him further.

"What is going on? I don't under–"

Eugene took out a large, curved blade, and his face changed so suddenly Gus barely saw the flicker between Eugene's smile and Eugene's cocky grimace.

"No!" Gus cried.

Eugene sliced the blade through the throat of his wife.

"No!" Gus cried again, and tried to move, but his feet were stuck, he couldn't, wasn't able, immobile, frantically so, stood in position like nails were digging through his feet and screwing him into the floor.

Eugene sliced open Laney's chest and Gus could swear he saw the last few beats of her heart hesitantly throbbing.

"Please, stop..." Gus whimpered, still trying to move but to no avail.

Eugene stepped toward Whizzo and sliced his throat.

"Honestly, Gus," Donny said. "Stop it, you're making a scene."

"Leave them alone!"

Desert was next. She didn't even struggle.

Donny stood.

He had a blade too.

"What?" Gus said.

And, just as Donny struck Gus with the blade, Gus awoke, sweating and screaming.

Chapter Two

Gus was suddenly cold.

His face could fill a bucket with the sweat amassing on his forehead. His heart was bursting against his ribs, his breath was wheezing, and his hands were clammy.

But any heat he was feeling whilst asleep abruptly left as he adjusted to the cold, early morning air.

He looked around at what seemed to be a wooden cabin, and he remembered stopping here for the night. At an abandoned wooden shack in the middle of a field. To rest. To recuperate.

Maybe this used to be a farm. A year or so ago, the fields would have been full of crops instead of dead weeds. Full of cows and pigs instead of burnt out carcasses. Happy ramblers walking across the country rather than fading infected, desperate for something to quell their starving appetite.

Now what?

There was a hazy amber glow outside the window. The window was painted in smudges and moss was engrained in its corners, but he could still just about make out the light.

Desert sat at the window, staring out of it, gun in hand. It was her turn to take watch; not that she could see much out of the filthy glass – but he had a feeling that, although she was staring outside, she probably had no conscious awareness of what she was looking at. She looked to be lost, her mind elsewhere, a vague alertness about her. She cradled the gun like a cat sat on her knee, and he half-expected her to start stroking it.

He looked down.

Sadie.

Asleep. Her hand on his right knee.

Just below her head was his artificial leg. A spring Whizzo had created for him that meant he could not only walk again, but propel himself forward into a run.

Clever kid, that Whizzo.

Speaking of which...

He looked around. Whizzo was in the far corner, tinkering with some kind of appliance. Gus couldn't tell what it was, but he rarely could – Whizzo was good with gadgets and all that stuff, and Gus didn't even attempt to interfere.

If Gus was the muscle of the situation, Whizzo was quite clearly the brains.

He put his hand on Sadie's cheek and gently ran it down her hair. She shifted, a cheeky smile and a happy flicker of her sleeping eyes. She was like a pet. Somewhere inside of her was the zombie gene – but it was somewhere deep and buried. Gus trusted Sadie more than anyone. She was unable to communicate or function as a person could, speaking in few syllables – but he knew she understood.

Plus, she was the best fighter they had, and she was the only one of them who could survive the blood of the infected. To a regular person, just a speck of blood between their lips and they would be trying to eat their friend's flesh within minutes.

But not Sadie.

Sadie was special.

Then there was Desert. Still preoccupied with her thoughts. She'd barely said a word to Gus since their confrontation with Donny a few weeks ago.

Donny, who was once the biggest irritation in Gus's life – but ended up, along with Sadie, saving him from his own depression. After the death of his family the only thing he'd looked forward to was the sweet relief of suicide, but Donny and Sadie had shown him nothing but unconditional caring. Something he had not expected.

But something had been done to Donny by the prime minster, Eugene Squire, the head of his army, General Boris Hayes, and their team of scientists. Something that had involved warping Donny's mind and turning him into a cross between the infected and a human – but not in the way that Sadie was.

Donny had become so much worse.

Donny had become what the zombie gene was intended for in the first place. A ruthless killer, stronger and quicker than the average person.

Gus had only just managed to escape death by Donny's hand himself.

But Prospero, Desert's friend, had not been so lucky. And, in that way, Gus could understand her frustration. Could understand her anger.

Hell, look what happened to him when he lost those he loved. He'd spent six months drinking himself to death, just waiting for the right moment.

But Gus had a feeling Desert's constant bad mood was something more than that. That there was some deeper resentment in her mind.

He wasn't sure how bothered he was about finding out what it was. If it would help her to get it out in the open, great – but if it made her reckless, he'd rather she just let it go, got on with it, and focussed on their mission.

"It's time to go," Desert announced.

Gus woke Sadie up gently, and they all readied themselves.

Preparing to re-enter the facility.

The place where Gus, Sadie and Donny had been taken prisoner and tortured for months.

Now it was abandoned and overrun with the infected.

But it was time they had answers.

They needed to find out what had happened to Donny. They needed to know what Eugene Squire was doing.

And in the remnants of the facility were the answers they were looking for.

Chapter Three

❧❧❧

They walked as they always did. Gus leading the front, followed by Desert and Sadie, and Whizzo lagging behind.

Gus considered talking to Desert. Walking slowly until he was beside her and asking her what was troubling her.

But what was the point?

He'd just get the same response he'd received the last time he tried, and the time before that, and the time before that.

A barely inaudible grunt of "nothing."

Honestly, if that was how she was going to be, he wasn't that bothered. He wasn't inclined to waste his time knocking on a door that had evidently been shut, locked and bolted.

So he let his mind wander.

And he thought about something he had been thinking about a lot over the last few days.

Donny.

Whether he stood a chance against him, and what he would even do if he did.

Donny was evidently part of whatever Eugene Squire was

planning. The question wasn't whether or not a confrontation with Donny was inevitable – it was what their approach to that confrontation was going to be once it happened.

The obvious solution had presented itself to Gus, albeit very briefly – killing him. But this solution was dismissed in the very same thought.

Donny had done for Gus what no one else could. He'd helped him find purpose. And Gus did not wish to repay that by ending the guy's life.

So what then?

The next question was whether or not there was an element of humanity left in Donny.

Whether there was something left to save.

Whether the old Donny was still there.

And this led Gus to think back to their previous fight, to think about how Donny could have killed Gus – but didn't.

Why didn't he?

Another memory abruptly presented itself to Gus's thoughts, in the way that memories so often do. A journey from the deep subconscious forced to the forefront of his mind like a punch through a brick wall.

Back when they were driving together, just after meeting Sadie...

Sunglasses.

Or *shades* as Donny had so uncoolly termed them.

Donny had moaned about how he'd been desperate for a cool set of shades. That he'd always wanted them.

Gus had retrieved some for him from a shop he looted. A way of apologising for his snappy manner, for being the person he was.

Donny had bloody loved those shades.

Sunglasses, Gus reminded himself. *Don't start calling them shades too...*

That person had to still be there.

Didn't he?

They approached a small cluster of zombies, all gathered around an open corpse, feeding like hyenas in a zoo.

Gus looked at them, knowing they were once people; maybe even with a humorous nature or naïve sensibilities like Donny.

Now look at them.

Brainless. Numb. Dead.

And Gus's hope diminished.

It wasn't like he was about to reason with these infected.

No – he was going to kill them.

Was Donny any different?

He dropped his head. A pain ran from the back of his skull to his forehead and stayed there, resting like a laser beam piercing into his brain. The whole situation was one giant migraine.

"No guns," Gus said to no one in particular. "We don't want to attract anymore."

Gus took out a broad machete, presented it, and clanged it against his aesthetic foot. Desert took out a similar weapon, Sadie readied her hands, and Whizzo backed away.

The infected turned and promptly ran toward them.

Gus lunged his weapon into the cranium of one, Desert into the head of another – and Sadie dispatched another three in half the time; swiping her nails like claws through their heads and removing them from their bodies.

Gus looked back at Whizzo, who was shaking.

"You all right?" Gus asked.

Whizzo nodded.

Gus put his hand affectionately on the back of Sadie's neck and smiled at her. She smiled back.

Finally, he turned to Desert.

"Are you okay?"

"Fine," she answered, and continued walking.

By the time the sun had reached the highest point in the sky they had approached broken fences, and the daunting task began to loom over them like the darkened buildings of the facility.

BEFORE

Chapter Four

The fire was lit, the television was off, and the moon
was placed perfectly in the sky.

Laney sat neatly in her father's arms, like a circle
nestled flawlessly inside a bigger circle. Her eyelids were
drooping but she refused to let them close, and refused to let
her dad know, for fear that the moment would end and the
announcement that it was time for bed would be made.

"Have you not had enough yet?" Gus asked, though there
was nothing in his voice that suggested he wanted the moment
to end either. The bounce to his pitch was playful, and his arms
were wrapped in a warm snuggle around Laney.

"No! More!" she requested.

"Fine, fine," Gus said, smiling warmly. "What shall we read
next?"

Laney stretched from the armchair to the bookcase. She
found a book that was way too big for her and pulled it out. Its
corners were turned up, the edges scuffed and scrapes of the
tatty image on the cover were missing.

"This one?" Gus said. "Really?"

"Yes!"

"I'm not sure. I think this book is more meant for big girls. Maybe in a few years' time."

"No! This one!"

He sighed, taking the book and looking over it. He didn't recall ever purchasing or acquiring this book. Maybe it was one of Janet's.

"But what if you don't understand what's going on? What if you don't know what's happening?"

Laney shrugged. Like it mattered!

"Okay, if you're sure."

She gave a little cheer and placed the entire weight of her head on his chest; which was hard and muscly, but to her, was always soft.

Gus tried to read the title on the cover, but it had been destroyed beyond legibility. Instead, he opened it, and looked at the title written in Times New Roman upon the front page.

The Ever-present.

Where had this book come from? What even was it?

Ah well, if that's what she's asked for...

He flicked the pages to chapter one.

"It was a tough day," Gus began. "But it was never tough enough for Roy. He could take a cast-iron morning and turn it into a fluffy afternoon. His hands were rough from working, and his belly hard from drinking, but underneath, his soul was as elegant and beautiful as a soul ever could be."

He glanced at Laney, knowing full well that she was not picking up on any of the nuances of the language he was delivering. Still, she remained engrossed and enthralled, gripped to every strange word.

"Are you sure about this?" he checked.

"Carry on, Daddy, carry on!"

"Okay," he said, and kept on reading. "He worked hard day and night. Tooth and nail, as his old man would say – though his teeth were sparse and his nails broken. Still, he worked tooth and nail, as it is said, until he had enough to provide his children with central heating and a holiday and a puppy and every other pleasure he could dote upon them."

Her eyelids were drooping, he could see that – but she did all she could to fight it. So he kept going.

And he kept going.

And he kept going.

Eventually, he had to take her to bed. She had entered the realm of dreams and there was no way she could have continued to fight it. He gave her a kiss on the forehead, whispered *good night,* and turned the light off as he left.

He asked his wife, later that evening, whether she had bought this book. Janet said that she didn't recall. She chuckled when Gus mentioned that Laney insisted on having it read to her. Glancing over the first few pages, she acknowledged how big some of the words were and descriptive some of the language was – but, nevertheless, Laney requested the same book again the following night.

And the following night.

And the night after that.

And the night after that, and after that, and after that.

Until she no longer had to request it, and Gus was automatically awaiting her in the evening with the book in his hand and his lap empty.

It took months to get through it.

And Gus was positive she didn't understand a word.

But she loved her father's reading voice; if warmth was a sound, that was how it would be.

But, several months after the first word had been spoken, the conclusion to Roy's story came about and she was sad to hear it.

But that book became Gus's favourite.

He read it again himself a few months later, when he was

stationed in Afghanistan – as if reading it somehow made him closer to his daughter.

He returned with the book even more tatty than it had been to begin with, but he returned with it nonetheless – in fact, he treasured it more than he treasured his water or his packets of food or his gun that defended him against the enemy.

Until the day came that Gus was discharged, just before the infection broke out in London.

Then the book was the last thing he thought about, and it was left behind with his family.

AFTER

Chapter Five

The infected, when left unstimulated, were odd – even odder than they were when running at you with their jaws snapping, eyes wide and decaying fingers outstretched. They were usually a terrifying sight, so to see so many standing dormant around the circumference of the facility appeared, in the only way Gus could describe it, odd.

"What do we do?" Whizzo asked, remaining behind the others. They all lay flat out on their bellies, beside the broken-down fences, watching whilst staying invisible.

Gus could probably count twenty-something. It wasn't the greatest number of them he'd ever faced, but it was still not an ideal task.

"So where is it we need to go?" Gus asked, as if it would somehow help him to come up with a clear plan.

"The office of Doctor Janine Stanton," Whizzo replied. "We think it's either on the first or second floor."

"Of which building?"

"I don't know."

There were five or six buildings, each of them large and foreboding. This didn't help.

"Sadie," Gus said. "You found Donny – which building was he in?"

She looked to Gus, her eyes resting on his for a moment, trying to figure out what he meant. She understood, it just took her a little longer.

Eventually, she raised an arm and directed it at the building furthest to the left.

"Brilliant." Gus turned to Whizzo. "And you're sure this is where we'll find stuff about what they did to Donny?"

"Sure?" Whizzo echoed, shrugging. "Is anyone ever really sure of anything anymore?"

Fair point.

Gus huffed. It was lucky, in a way, that the infected were all loitering in their own space, spread out sparsely over the terrain. This meant there were only a few they had to creep past.

Then again, they had no idea what quantity of infected were inside.

"Any ideas?" Gus asked Desert, hoping she was planning to be a little more helpful than she had been so far.

"Distraction?" she suggested. "One of us pulls them away as the rest of us enter."

"Nah, I'm not happy letting someone go off on their own."

She gave a wide-mouthed shrug, as if to say, *then what the hell did you ask me for?*

"Let's get as close as we can," Gus decided. "Come on."

He ignored Desert's glare. At no point had they decided that Gus would be leading them, and he knew it would just be another thing she would add to her list of resentments, but someone had to be decisive.

They stayed low as they crept around the circumference of the fallen fence. Gus never took his eyes off the infected. Every now and then, one of them would sniff, or snap their jaw, or twitch in their direction, and Gus would feel each of his limbs stiffen – all the limbs he had left, that is. But they were stealthy and silent, and they made it unnoticed to the fallen barrier about thirty or so yards away from the entrance – the door of which hung open like the gates of hell, leading them to a corridor of god-knows-what.

There were three infected lingering their way.

"Creep up behind and do it quietly, in synch. Understood?"

Sadie paused, then nodded.

Gus turned to Desert, who did not nod, but gave a petulant stare.

Whatever.

"On three," Gus decided. "One, two, three."

Remaining crouched, Desert, Sadie and Gus crept up behind one of the infected each. Following acknowledgement with brief eye contact, they disposed of their zombies – Desert and Gus with a knife to the head, and Sadie by scraping her nail along the infected's neck and pulling on their hair to remove their head. She appeared a little troubled by a wayward oesophagus that took an extra tug to separate from the body, but after an extra pull or two the head came off.

Gus looked around to see if they had attracted any attention, and kept looking as they made it to the door which was half-attached to the entrance, its glass shattered.

Gus nodded at Whizzo, who rushed to their side.

Gus looked around at the others, feeling a little nervous – which was odd, as he never felt nervous. This was his forte. War was his playground. He'd fought many powerful enemies and killed them without a second thought.

It was Desert.

She was making him uneasy.

In Afghanistan he knew his comrades would have his back.

Here, he had no idea. Whatever was going on inside her head was a mystery to Gus, and he was worried it was going to make her reckless.

"You cool?" he asked her.

"I'm fine," she replied.

He did not feel reassured.

"I'll take point," Gus said, and entered, slowly, calmly, knife ready in his right hand and his left resting on the gun attached to his hip.

The rest followed.

They were in.

Chapter Six

You cool?

He asks it like it's profound. Like a crap dad trying to be hip. Like it's something to like about him.

"I'm fine," she tells him, coldly, and intentionally so.

"I'll take point."

Of course you will.

Of course you damn well will.

Desert's fingers flexed and tightened.

Fool.

Every time he mentioned Donny it was in the same breath as ideas on how to save him.

Save him, oh let's save him, oh how can we save the homicidal freak who led them into a trap and killed Prospero?

They wouldn't save any of the other infected.

She grew fed up of her opinion being dismissed so many weeks ago that she had stopped voicing it, and decided to internalise it, to harness the anger like an untrained dog pulling on its lead.

So they were entering the facility.

Risking their lives to find research that would tell them what was done to Donny.

Research that, for Gus, would show them how to save him.

For her, it would show them how to kill him.

He's still good, still good, still so good, good left in him, oh so much good left in him.

Back when society was intact, you wouldn't have a murderer go on trial and be found guilty just to have the judge say *ah, well, there's still good in him.*

No.

You would lock him up.

If the death penalty existed in that judge's location, the idea would be vigorously entertained.

As far as she was concerned, Gus had gone past sense. Far past it. So much so, Gus was standing atop the cliff of irrationality and sense was too far below to even make out.

Desert did not intend to let Donny live.

But would she tell Gus that?

Would he listen?

And there he was, taking point. Leading. Like he was the one they should follow.

Like he was in Prospero's place.

Like he was in charge.

That decision had never been made. Had never been discussed nor decided.

Desert wasn't always the fiery warrior she had become. Once, she was Lucy Sanders. A timid secretary for Eugene Squire, working more hours than she should, being pushed and kicked around like it was all she was worth.

Then Eugene threatened her life and she escaped and she changed.

She grew a backbone. A heart. A fist she could punch with.

And never again – repeat, *never again* – would she be willing to let someone push her around or treat her as she was treated a year ago.

She would not let herself become the person she had been after battling so hard to become the person she had become.

They approached a corner in the corridor. Gus raised his right arm and closed his fist. Typical army sign for *stop*.

Why should she stop?

Why should she ever do what he tells her?

She saved Gus.

Never forget that, you one-legged bastard.

She. Saved. Gus.

He ran – or hopped – from the facility, and fell into one of her traps.

She took him in.

With Whizzo.

With Prospero.

They gave him his artificial leg, rehabilitated him, gave him a purpose.

It was him that owed her, not the other way around.

Never the other way around.

Gus rushed from the corner of the corridor and she heard a gentle slice and the crack of bone. He reappeared and waved them to follow him, and they kept moving, stepping over the body of an infected as they did.

They turned another corner, disposed of more infected, and an office appeared with a proud plaque on the door reading *Dr Janine Stanton*.

They were going to find out what Donny was.

His strengths.

His weaknesses.

And she planned to use both of those against him – whether Gus agreed with her or not.

Chapter Seven

W hizzo wasn't sure what he was looking for; but he was sure, as the saying goes, that he would know when he found it.

"Make it quick, kid," Gus instructed, standing at the door, gun in hand, looking back and forth.

"Want a hand?" Desert asked.

"Er, yeah..." responded Whizzo. "Just find anything that looks like research, I guess."

He opened his rucksack and withdrew a few more rucksacks, one that he tossed to Desert, and one that he tossed to Sadie. Sadie looked blankly at the bag and back to Whizzo, but as soon as Whizzo began shoving wayward bits of paper into his bag, she soon learnt what she needed to do and copied.

The laboratory was quite small. There was a chair with restraints that one could be fixed to, though those restraints were broken. Pieces of paper were strewn across the floors and walls, and there were streams of blood decorating the surfaces.

He glanced at a few sheets as he pushed them into his bag, being hasty but curious. There was what looked like first-hand accounts, like journals, on many of the sheets. Some others contained formulas and ingredients, and he was sure he saw *blood of the infected* listed amongst them.

He ransacked a few cupboards and a few drawers, pulling out wads of paper and shovelling them in. He came to a glass cabinet above a set of drawers containing beakers.

He wanted to know what was in them; but then again, he didn't.

Should he take them with him?

Would it be a risk?

Could they be hazardous?

"How much longer?" Gus asked.

"Not long. A minute."

He several, wrapped them in a few pieces of paper, and placed them in his bag.

"Desert," said Gus, alert to something he'd seen. She put her rucksack on her back and followed him into the corridor.

Whizzo heard a few grunts and a few slices and, a few moments later, they returned, their blades slightly bloody.

"We need to go," Gus said, blankly.

Sadie walked up to Whizzo, showing him her bag, like a child seeking reassurance from their teacher.

"Great," Whizzo said, not really sure what he was supposed to say. But it seemed to satisfy her.

He put his bag on and she copied him.

"Okay," Whizzo said to Gus.

Gus paused, something on a desk catching his attention. He walked over to it.

It was a framed photo.

"What?" Whizzo asked.

Gus turned the photo toward Whizzo. It was a woman, with a child sat playing on the floor beside her. The woman was smiling.

"Think this was her?" Gus mused. "Think this was Doctor Janine Stanton?"

Whizzo shrugged.

"Could have been."

Gus nodded. For some reason he opened the frame, took the photo, and wedged it into his back pocket.

"Let's get out of here," he decided.

Chapter Eight

Gus wasn't entirely sure why he picked up the photograph. Maybe he wanted to know something more about this woman. Maybe it was part of the research. Or, maybe it was just morbid curiosity.

Either way, he could think about it later.

They kept low, Gus leading again, guiding them through the corridors, passing the bodies of the infected they had recently disposed of, heads open and faces unmoved.

Then they reached a corner of the corridor. Gus took a peek around it and halted, raising a hand to the others.

Shit.

How the hell had this happened?

They'd passed this corner to get here, and there had just been a few infected lurking that they had dispatched. Now the corridor was full. Groans filled the narrow walls, wandering bodies clattered into one another, and the smell of death hanging on the warm air suffocated them.

Every now and then, one of them sniffed.

And another one, and another one.

That's how...

They must have smelt them. With months of the potent odour of decay, the introduction of four fresh bodies must have stuck out.

"What is it?" Desert asked.

"Come look," he told her.

She crept to his side and peered around the corner, quickly withdrawing once she'd seen them.

"Where did they come from?" she said.

Gus huffed.

"No idea."

He turned back to the other two.

Could Sadie take them down?

He struggled to see how many there were, but there were a lot. So many that they couldn't move without barging into others. So many he couldn't see the other side of the corridor. So many that there was no way of knowing.

"Could we take them?" Desert suggested.

Gus really didn't want to dismiss another of her ideas, knowing how much she seemed to dislike him at the moment, but there was no way they could take on that many in this enclosed space and make it out alive.

"I don't think we can," Gus responded.

"What then?" Desert said petulantly. "This is the way out."

"There must be another way out."

"Where? This building could easily be half a mile long."

"Look at them, Desert. You know how fast they are, how strong they are – what do you want us to do?"

"Sadie could–"

"Sadie doesn't have enough space to..."

Gus stopped. Hesitated. Now wasn't the time.

"We go back on ourselves then," Desert said, resolved.

Gus was relieved that the argument wasn't going any further. Now they could just focus solely on getting out.

Gus turned to Whizzo and Sadie.

"We go the other way," he told them.

They turned and began to step as lightly as they could, so the sounds of their feet on the floor were barely taps.

Gus could still hear the infected groaning and growling, their jaws still snapping, their shuffles uncoordinated and senseless.

Gus put his finger over his mouth to signal to Sadie to be quiet, then pointed over her shoulder. She nodded, turned, and led the line.

Gus took his gun from his belt, ready; just in case.

Though he wouldn't need it.

They were nearly far enough away that they couldn't be heard.

At least, that's what Gus thought, just as Whizzo knocked into the door to Janine Stanton's office that he'd left ajar, forcing it to thwack against the wall and reverberate numerous times around the corridor.

Chapter Nine

Whizzo wondered if he'd ever get used to the concept of running from zombies. Yes, they were the infected, and zombie was a term put on them by humans – but the situation was just as absurd as it was in trashy horror films and comics that he used to read.

One thing that he could definitely never get used to, however – despite it being a common occurrence – was him being at fault for them having to run from zombies.

For all he knew, his own stupidity had just cost them all their lives.

He ran as fast as he could, but still ended up at the rear of the group. Desert hung back, constantly urging him to hurry up, but he was hurrying as fast as he could. He was heaving and panting and limping and pushing and doing all he could to not give up and just let them all eat him.

He could feel their breath on the back of his neck.

He could feel the reach of their hands.

The only thing that was preventing them from getting him was their speed – sounds peculiar, but the corridor had many twists and turns, and the infected were running with such acceleration and ferocity that at every turn they skidded into one another.

At the head of the group, Gus drew his gun and aimed it at a far window.

Gus had been very strict in his insistence that they not use their guns – they would attract more infected.

Whizzo supposed that instruction was useless now.

Gus shot out the glass and dove through it.

Sadie followed.

"Come on!" Desert urged.

"I'm fine, you go," Whizzo asserted, despite being terrified and not fine and fully sure that he was going to be eaten.

Desert leapt out of the window and reached her hand in for Whizzo.

But Whizzo was Whizzo, and just as he approached the window he stumbled over his own feet and collapsed on the floor.

"No!" Desert shouted, but Whizzo barely heard it above the moans.

He turned and looked at the approaching infected.

Barging against the wall, against each other, in sheer desperation, hungry for him.

He pushed himself up and went to hurl himself out of the window, but it was too late – one of them had a hold of his foot.

"Get down!" screamed Gus.

Whizzo ducked beneath the window and looked up at the face of the nearest infected. It leapt at him with its yellow, gangrenous teeth dripping drool over its prey.

A gunshot overtook the sound of the infected and that zombie fell to the ground.

A stream of bullets continued, and the infected closest to him fell, and the infected behind them stumbled over the bodies.

This didn't deter them as, even though they were stranded on the floor, they still reached and clutched at Whizzo's leg.

"Desert!" he heard Gus shout. "Come on!"

Even more bullets came flying through the window.

It was a smart move, Whizzo decided. Even though there were so many of them, they were all in a confined space, condensed together, and a constant stream of bullets at head height would stop more of them than if they were in open ground.

It was a smart idea.

A smart idea Whizzo would never have thought of.

He watched the infected as they locked eyes with him, reached out, then collapsed. One-by-one they fell, flailing arms and desperate lunges.

They were so strong, so quick – but Gus was Gus, and he knew how to fight.

Whizzo had never been in a fight in his life that he hadn't run from.

He had enough of looking at them. The constant gun sounds were making his brain feel like it was throbbing against his skull, and the sight of them going from dead to deader was becoming all the more disgusting and disturbing by the second.

He bowed his head.

Buried it in his arms and between his knees.

He wouldn't be able to see if one of them made it to him.

Then again, what if he could see? What then?

There was no running. No fighting.

Just being useless, as always...

He sighed.

His forehead pulsated, sore under the strain of his incoming migraine.

What if one of them got to him?

What if he was about to die?

What if he wasn't around to help the resistance fight the infected and fight Eugene Squire?

No one would ever notice...

If his contribution wasn't there, no one would contemplate his input.

What even was his contribution?

He made more gadgets than he could keep track of, and tinkered with technology to little avail – just because he was so keen for a purpose.

But, truth was, they were having to rescue him.

Again.

The bullets ceased

He opened his eyes.

A pile of corpses sat atop one another in front of him like a wall of death.

"Come on!" he heard Desert's voice urge him.

He stood, peering over the window. There they were, guns slightly lowered, awaiting him.

He went to climb out.

But something stopped him. He was over the window pane, and something had his arm.

He looked back.

One of the infected, squished beneath a mass of bodies, had a hold of his hand.

"Come on!"

He thought that was Desert's voice. He couldn't be sure.

He just knew, there and then, that it was over.

The infected grabbed onto his little finger, clamping down with its teeth.

Someone pulled him, trying to grab him away from the infected, but its jaw was fixed and it was not moving.

"Move!" came Gus's gruff voice.

Gus appeared beside Whizzo, wielding a knife.

Before Whizzo had any idea what was happening, Gus had swung the knife downwards and sliced through Whizzo's little finger.

The last thing Whizzo saw before he passed out was the infected munching and swallowing that precious little muscle.

Chapter Ten

✿❦✿

All the scientists at the compound knew the sound of Eugene Squire's heavy breathing. It hung over their shoulder as he nosed at their work, loud and stinking of fish.

As head scientist, Doctor Charles Moore knew this sound better than anyone else. He'd had to be the one communicating with Eugene on behalf of his team for the past few weeks, and it was already a job he greatly disliked. He wondered how Doctor Janine Stanton had managed to do it for so long.

And that was the thought that kept him going – Janine Stanton.

He did not want to end up sharing her fate.

They all clung onto the idea of someday seeing their families again, though none of them knew if their loved ones were even still alive. They had never left the facility, and they were never permitted to leave the new compound either.

None of them knew what they were really creating.

But Charles did.

Oh, boy, Charles did.

He'd seen them. Below. Training. Readying themselves.

He'd rather run from the compound and face all of the infected than face a few of those monsters.

"A word," Eugene hissed over his shoulder.

Charles looked back at his colleagues, noticing a few hesitant glances. He gave a faint nod as he was led out of the laboratory and into the corridor.

"I'm getting impatient," Eugene announced, his voice as smug and posh as a smug, posh voice could sound.

He was a puny man who walked around with an upper-class arrogance. Charles could take him, his colleagues could take him – hell, even the rats that scuttled past their feet could take him.

But none of them dared.

It would be so easy. Just throw him to the infected. Stick a needle in his neck. Break a beaker and slit his throat with broken glass.

But the authority this little man with his disjointed walk had was ridiculous.

Take General Boris Hayes away, take his army away, and he'd be nothing... I'd have him then...

"But – but you have your army," Charles said. "I've seen them below. They are – they are strong. They will fight for you."

"They will, they will," Eugene confirmed, placing a hand on Charles's shoulder with what Eugene probably intended to be a firm grip. "But I want more, Charles. I want *more*."

"We – we're working as best as we can."

Eugene laughed. A patronising chuckle that would be too patronising for even the most petulant of children.

"No," Eugene decided. "You're not."

Eugene leant in further.

"The army is beautiful, you are right there," he said, his voice low. "I love them. I love them to bits, as if they were my own. I can't wait to see them fight, to see them kill and maim and–" He gripped Charles's shoulder tighter. "Eat and feed. But I want more."

"More?" Charles echoed.

"They will fight and they will win. But I don't want to have to wait for the carnage to be over, I want it to be instant."

"I – I don't understand..."

"Of course you don't."

Eugene smiled a fake smile, a sinister smile, a smile with hostility and sadism behind it.

"I want them better."

"Better?"

Eugene nodded. "*Better.*"

"I – we – we are trying."

Eugene shook his head.

"I don't think you're trying hard enough."

"We are."

"Well, I'll tell you what. My army, they – they need to feed. Don't they? After all, we all feed."

"Y – yes."

"What do they feed on?"

"...Us."

Eugene nodded.

"That, my friend," Eugene said, pronouncing every syllable, "is why you need to increase your efforts. Or you will find your team of scientists depleting in quantity quite rapidly."

"Please, we are–"

Eugene pulled a *zippit* sign across his lips.

"Less talky, more doey."

Charles nodded.

What he'd give.

Just an uppercut, a smack in that smug face, a headbutt on that incredulous set of nostrils.

"I want them faster. I want them bigger. I want them *better*."

Charles nodded.

"Go. Now."

Charles backed away, back into the laboratory.

The rest of the scientists didn't speak. They didn't need to.

Charles's increased work rate told them everything they needed to know about how the conversation had gone.

BEFORE

Chapter Eleven

His wife. His childhood sweetheart. The woman he had loved since he was sixteen.

Clambering toward him. Demonic eyes, snapping jaw, her joints twisting in the wrong directions.

He slid his knife into the base of his wife's skull.

His daughter. Probably killed by her mother. Legless, dragging herself toward him.

He couldn't bring himself to do it.

But he had to.

He knew he had to.

Hell, even this horrid creature masquerading as his daughter knew it – but that didn't make it any easier.

He crouched beside her.

Don't do this.

He wiped his eyes on his sleeve.

Don't do this.

He looked into her eyes, those empty, angry eyes, the bloodshot cuticles that glared at him with such vacancy he could barely take it.

Don't. Do. This.

He did it.

He drove his knife into the back of her skull.

And he looked at the damage he'd done. The mess he'd made.

Why hadn't he arrived in time?

Not that he knew when *in time* would have been.

They could have been like this for hours.

He'd rushed back from town, ignoring the casualties, weaving his motorbike in and out of those oncoming... things...

But he realised now what he'd known before he had even arrived.

It was too late.

It would forever be too late.

And though he was still alive, a piece of him had been bitten off and left with them.

A racket announced itself downstairs. The door barging open, swaying wrathfully against its hinges.

The snarls.

The stink.

The chaos.

He'd been around enough dead bodies to know the smell – he knew it all too well. But those bodies that smelt so bad had never stood up and attacked him.

He heard them. At the bottom steps. Bashing each other out of the way. Knocking into one another to get to Gus first.

He remained at the top of the stairs, his family a bloody mess, inside out, scattered around his knees.

He had to move. If he wanted to live, he had to move.

Then again...

Do I want to live?

What would be the purpose?

The point?

The function?

Their feet bashed against the steps, coming toward him so

fast, yet it didn't feel so fast, it felt drawn-out, slow motion, like a film moving frame by frame.

He stood. Forced his heavy feet to wade into the bedroom.

And he saw it.

On the bookcase.

The Ever-present.

He took the book and threw it against the wall. He tore off the cover, the back cover, pulled at the spine, ripped out the pages. He did not stop until the room was littered with fallen pieces of fading, inked paper.

They entered the bedroom.

He ran to the window and leapt, landing atop the conservatory below. He slid down the glass roof and into the garden, landing painfully on his arm.

They must have heard him, as the garden was suddenly filled with them, streaming through the broken fence like water through a dam.

He sprinted to the fence and jumped, pulling himself up and landing in the garden of the next house over.

They didn't seem to be able to jump the fence.

They could eat his neighbours, almost match the speed of a car, and kill his family – but they couldn't leap a fence.

What the fuck is going on?

He kept running.

Leapt over another fence and landed in the adjacent field.

He paused.

Looked back at the bedroom window of his house.

What *used to be* his house.

Another step and the bedroom window would be out of sight.

His family would be gone.

Never buried. Left to rot in the hallway.

Decaying among pages of an awful book he had truly grown to treasure.

I love you.

His parting thought was interrupted by more snarls and he turned, and he ran, and he hid.

And, though he hung around in an alcoholic stupor for months afterwards, waiting for the right moment to die – he never forgot the sight of those faces.

He would always be a father – just a father without a daughter.

AFTER

Chapter Twelve

Whizzo awoke, sweating as he expected to be craving flesh.

He hadn't any idea what it was like to be one of the infected, and he'd imagined that he would be far more absentminded than this; so, as thoughts rushed into his mind like water beating down a dam, he realised that he wasn't infected.

And he realised that he wasn't alone.

His feet hung off the end of a bumpy mattress in what he assumed was a child's bedroom; what with the bright pink walls and the assortment of cuddly toys that were either destroyed or crusted with old blood.

"God, tell me this is a nightmare," he said.

Desert smiled. She arose from her seat in the corner of the room and meandered to his bedside, perching on what little of the bed was left to perch on.

"Honestly," she said, a slanted smirk etching toward her cheek, "I think it suits you."

He tried sitting up, only to find his back in incredulous amounts of pain.

"How long?" Whizzo inquired.

"Not long," she answered. "About a day."

He nodded. Looked around again.

Pieces of battered toy horse lay across the floor, torn children's books were left discarded on a beaten bookcase against the far wall, and the curtains, decorated with unicorns, were so ripped that it looked as if those unicorns had been savagely slaughtered.

"A whole day, and this is what you came up with?"

She chuckled.

"You know you lost it, right?"

"Lost what?"

She raised her eyebrows.

It took a few moments to understand what she meant. Then the memory came back.

He looked down. There, on his left hand, was a bandage covering the stump of a missing little finger.

It surprised him to find that he didn't miss it that much. He could hardly complain to Gus about it – what with him missing a leg. Compared to that this was spilt milk. Tempestuously exploding, stormy spilt milk.

"You okay?" Desert asked.

He stared at his finger. Or, at least, the lack of it.

"Yeah," he decided. "It's not a big loss, is it? People have lost more."

"It's just a good job you're not a lefty."

"You kidding? I'd give my right arm to be ambidextrous."

Desert snorted a laugh. "The nineties called, they want their joke back," she teased, and he joined in the laughter.

The laughter was quickly halted by a set of thudding footsteps.

"Thought I heard voices," said Gus as he entered. "Sorry for the room, was the only one not covered in blood and shit."

Whizzo forced a smile, ignoring how deadly cold Desert had suddenly become.

"Time to get up then, mate," Gus urged. "Need to make sense of the stuff we found."

"He's only just woken up," Desert protested. "Give him a minute."

"Fine," Gus answered. "Have a minute. I'll be downstairs."

He left, leaving Desert shaking her head and narrowing her eyes into an intense glare.

"He's right, you know," said Whizzo. "We don't know how much time we have."

Desert grimaced; a mixture of annoyance at Gus, and annoyance at Whizzo's acknowledgement of Gus's correctness.

"He still doesn't need to be a dick about it."

Whizzo sighed. He turned his legs and pushed himself out of bed. Desert went to help him, but he waved his arm to stop her.

Desert had left a set of clothes out for him. Not in great condition, but no bloodstains – which was probably the best he could hope for.

He put them on.

"You know," he said, doing up his belt, "whatever this is, going on with Gus... You have to quit it."

"There's nothing going on with–"

"Oh, give it a break." He turned toward her and placed his hands on his hips. "You've been giving him the evil eye every chance you get. I see it. He sees it. Hell, even Sadie probably bloody sees it."

"Yeah, well," was all she could muster.

"We need to work together."

"But it's not that simple, is it?"

"I don't know, see, because I don't know what your problem is."

Desert's arms folded and her glare turned to Whizzo.

"We lost Prospero and you can't figure it out?"

He stopped moving. Leant against the wall. Huffed. Bowed his head.

She had a point.

Not a helpful one, but she had one.

"I hate what happened to Prospero," admitted Whizzo. "Then again, there's a lot of things I hate. But there's no way Gus could have known."

"And say we are confronted with Donny again, and he kills one of us. What do you think Gus would do to Donny then? Would he be prepared to stop him?"

He gave a big, non-committal shrug.

"I don't know, Desert. I don't know. Why don't you try asking him?"

She went to object, but he stopped her.

"Either way, it needs to stop."

She went to object again, but he opened the door and walked out.

"I have work to do," he told her as he left.

Chapter Thirteen

✦✦✦

Gus left Whizzo to work as he went in search of water, and it didn't take him long until he found a nearby stream. The house was still visible behind him, though 'house' was a loose term; it was barely a shack. Unfortunately, they hadn't the luxury of fussiness as they'd fled the facility, what with an unconscious Whizzo over his shoulder.

He held the container under the water for long enough for it to fill to the brim. He lifted it to his dry, cracked lips and relished the feel of water plunging down his throat. The water was by no means clean and did not taste at all sanitary – but one learns to live with the provisions they have, and he was grateful for it.

He refilled the container and trudged back to the house. He entered to find Whizzo sat at a table with pieces of paper scattered across it. Gus would offer to help, as he was sure Desert would – but this was not their area of expertise. He was far better at the fighting and the killing, and all these notes would mean very little to him.

Sadie was cuddled up in a ball in the corner of the room with her eyes closed. How she could nap so easily Gus did not know. He woke her briefly to give her some water, for which she was grateful, then she went straight back to sleep.

He passed the water to Whizzo, who drank it in gulps before resuming his work.

Next, he looked around for Desert.

"Where's Desert?" he asked.

"Here," came a voice and she emerged in the doorway.

Gus handed her the container, watching her warily as he did.

"Cheers," she said, and took a few large swigs of water.

"Hey, Gus," Whizzo said.

"Yeah?"

"Desert wanted to talk to you about something."

Gus turned to Desert. She huffed and shot Whizzo a look that clearly said *thanks, dickhead.*

"What?" Gus prompted.

Desert said nothing. She went to speak, but she sighed and stopped herself.

"It's about Donny," Whizzo said.

"Donny?" Gus repeated. "What about him?"

Desert shook her head, refusing to engage.

"Desert has been a bitch toward you because she has a different opinion," Whizzo continued, prompting more angry glances from Desert. "Look, I'm just fed up of this, and want to get your grief sorted. You two need to work together, after all."

Whizzo looked to Gus, then to Desert, then resumed his work.

Damn, the kid was annoying – but the kid was also right.

"Come on then," said Gus. "He's got a point. What's going on?"

Desert shook her head and made her way across the room, as if to go do something, despite there being nothing for her to do.

"Stop walking away from me," Gus insisted. "You are doing my nut in. Either tell me what's going on, or..."

"Or what?"

Gus met her glare.

"Or piss off. You're not doing any of us any favours."

"That's the thing, though, isn't it? It's not like I can say what's on my mind. To you, it's not even a discussion."

"This about Donny?"

"Yeah."

"Then what is there to discuss?"

Desert huffed. For a second, she looked as if she was about to answer. Instead, she turned her head away and shook it, biting her lip.

"Spit it out," Gus insisted.

"So, say we find Donny, yeah?"

"We will find Donny."

"Okay, so when we do find him – what then?"

Gus frowned. He didn't understand her point.

"What do you mean, what then?"

"Well, what happens when we find him?"

"We take him. We capture him back from Eugene Squire and we undo whatever was done to him."

She shook her head with even more vigour.

"So we save him, yeah?" she said, her speech getting quicker and more full of spite. "You're saying we should save him?"

"Of course."

"Have you forgotten what he did?"

"What do you mean what he–"

"I'm talking about killing Prospero. You may not have known him for long, but Prospero was our friend, and I miss him. And Donny led us all into a trap and killed him."

"And I'm sorry for that happening."

"Say one of *our* friends dragged you into a trap, and it was *Sadie* who was killed – what then?"

Gus looked to Sadie, whose head roused for a moment, then sunk back into her nap.

"I don't get what you're saying," Gus said, even though he did; he just wanted to hear her say it.

"I'm questioning whether Donny is someone we save. Or whether it's someone we..."

"What?"

She looked to the floor.

"What? Go on, say it."

"Kill."

Gus paced, his fingers digging into his palm, attacked by a scurry of poisonous thoughts. He willed himself to think clearly, to think straight – but his mind was a sudden mess, and he struggled to contain that mess from spilling out of his mouth.

"I know it's not what you want to hear," Desert said.

"You don't have any fucking idea what I want to hear," Gus barked, saliva bursting from beneath his teeth with each plosive.

"But let me just ask you a question, yeah?"

It was Gus's turn to shake his head. He did not stop pacing.

"If he was bitten by one of the infected, and started to turn – what would you do?"

"What?"

"You heard me."

Gus did not want to answer.

"I don't know what that has to do with anything."

"My point is," Desert began, stepping forward, growing in confidence, "that you would not go out there and try and reason with one of the infected. You wouldn't go out there and try to compromise or talk them down. You'd kill them."

"It's not the same."

"But it is. He just has an enhanced version of the infection. He's still one of them."

Gus punched a glass cabinet, smashing it to a hundred

pieces. Shards of glass sprayed over his knuckles, cutting his hand, but he felt none of it. He did not care for the pain or for what the sound may have attracted. It was all he could do not to direct the fist at Desert.

Instead, he marched up to her, standing in her personal space, towering over her, and jabbed his finger with each word he said.

"We work together," he growled. "We fight together. We go down together. Fine. But let me make this clear – try to kill Donny, and I will kill you."

She said nothing. She didn't back off or step forward. She just stood there, looking up at his wounded visage.

"I repeat. I. Will. Kill. You."

They remained in that position for longer than was comfortable, neither being the first to move or step away.

Luckily for them, Whizzo was the one to break the confrontation.

"Guys," he said. "I think I have something."

Chapter Fourteen

Whizzo was grateful for the end of the argument. He was pleased they were talking through their issues, but the exchange had become less than productive.

"You want to hear it?" Whizzo prompted.

Both Gus and Desert approached the table, pausing at either side – avoiding eye contact and close proximity.

Sadie awoke, stretched, and sauntered over, also seemingly interested; despite how little she would probably understand.

"So it looks like the facility wasn't the only place they had labs," Whizzo said. "There's this compound, here, that I think they may be using."

He pointed to a map and noticed his missing finger again. He'd become so used to the constant stinging he'd forgotten it wasn't there, and the sight of it was a strange reminder that he'd never see that finger again.

"That's not far," Gus said. "A few miles, if that."

"Thing is, though, we might want to be careful," Whizzo said. In all honesty, he always wanted to be careful, and was dreading another fight, and was in two minds about whether to even reveal the next bit of information.

"What?" Gus prompted, awaiting Whizzo's further explanations.

Ah, well. Best get to it.

He pulled out a sheet of paper displaying an outline of a person and a list of chemicals.

"This is what I think they are trying to make."

"What is it?" Desert asked, peering over his shoulder and ignoring a scowl from Gus.

"It's... well, Donny. But not."

"What do you mean, but not?" Gus asked.

"As in, it's Donny, but... better."

"Better?"

"More powerful, I mean."

Gus grabbed the sheet and looked at it, as if it would mean anything to him.

"So you think..." Gus said, unable to order his thoughts.

Whizzo did it for him.

"I think Donny could just be the start. Maybe even a prototype."

"They are wanting to make more?"

Whizzo shrugged, leant back in his chair, and raised his hands indecisively.

"Could be. I don't know. Just hypothesising."

Gus rubbed his chin. Desert stood thoughtfully with her hands on her hips. Both of them looked at Whizzo, and still not at each other.

"And there's another thing. It keeps talking about a date that's around a week's time, probably less. I don't know what that is, but I think, in fact, I'm certain..."

Whizzo dreaded saying what he was about to say, but knew he had to say it anyway.

"I'm fairly positive," he continued, closing his eyes and

trying to think of any way he didn't have to say this, "that this is where we could find Donny."

"Are you certain?"

"Certain? No, I'm not certain of anything. But there's a link between the compound and this design, and this design involves Donny, and... Well, I think it's a pretty good shot."

Gus finally looked to Desert. She returned his stare. Both of them like two cats in an alleyway, suddenly alert to each other's presence.

"Do you think you coming is a good idea?" Gus asked her.

Desert scoffed. "I'm coming."

"Fine. But my instructions are clear."

"You're not the boss."

"We leave in the morning," Gus said, ignoring her comment. "It's starting to get dark and we need some rest. As soon as the sun's up, we go. Just to stake it out. No decisions yet, we need to see what we're dealing with."

He turned to Sadie, who was beaming up at him.

"Hear that?" he said. "Sun up, time to go. Yeah?"

She nodded.

He looked to the other two.

"I'm going to get some rest," he said, and charged out of the room. They heard his footsteps disappear upstairs.

"Well," Whizzo declared. "That could have gone better."

"He's full of shit."

"Is he?"

"Donny is infected."

"He's not one of the zombies, he's just got some of the zombie in him."

"So you're taking his side?"

Whizzo huffed and leant his face on his hands.

"I'm tired. I'm fed up. And I'm missing a finger. I don't care."

"You don't—"

"I hate what Donny did. I hate that Gus wants to save him. And I have no idea what's going to happen when – if – we find him. But for now, we do need some rest. Gus was at least right about that."

Desert looked to Whizzo like she had just been betrayed by her oldest friend; by a confidant she never thought would hurt her, yet had, deeply.

"Don't look at me like that," he told her. "You look sadder than my missing pinky."

She laughed.

They exchanged a smile.

Then she did as she was told and went to get some rest.

Chapter Fifteen

Through the corridors of the compound, past the turns and twists and up the lifts and through the doors, Eugene came to the room he often found himself arriving at in sleepless nights.

Not that there were many sleepless nights, mind – he slept soundly and peacefully, with his conscience clear and his dreams undisturbed.

But this night, he was awoken with a burning need to see them. To marvel once more at the creation that was going to set this world alight. The only sight that still captivated and enthralled him, despite the many, many times he had seen it.

He entered. Kept the light off – there was no need to announce his presence.

He made his way to the glass window that took up most of the wall, and looked down upon the vast, open room. It was like a hanger bay for aeroplanes, if they were to keep such things. But, instead of aeroplanes, there was a mass of bodies, all partaking in various activities.

One third of the room was enduring combat training. A piece of unguarded flesh was left to hang and they would fight one another to reach it first. Upon the sight of this piece of meat their bodies would become alert, turning feral, their eyes dilating, their movement ravenous, their drool seeping through the cracks of their stale teeth.

Along from that was the feeding bay. They had, at first, attempted to have them sit at tables and eat – but that had been a ridiculous expectation. Instead, they were put into a pen and left to devour the dispensed limbs or organs with little care for how much the others had.

And, in the final section of the grand space, was the obedience training.

After all, they couldn't let creatures this powerful off the figurative leash. They had to keep them trained and focussed, ready to attack on their command. Some less successful trainers had, unfortunately, not survived – but Eugene was still able to make use of their body parts in the feeding section.

He was surprised that the remaining trainers still did their job after learning this – but they knew what would happen if they didn't. It was either a possible death whilst training, or a certain death for refusing.

And this was the army the scientists had created for him. This was the enhanced gene. They had taken what they'd created with Donny, and made the army even more ruthless, more speedy, more hungry – and, overall, more lethal.

"Beautiful, ain't they?" came a familiar voice from across the room.

General Boris Hayes sat in the darkness, watching Eugene.

"Gosh, I did not see you there!"

"Thought you didn't."

"Can't sleep?"

"I rarely sleep. How can I when there's a sight like this to behold?"

Eugene nodded in agreement. They were quite something.

Hayes had remained as loyal as Eugene could ask for upon

discovering his plan – a plan that he was not initially privy to. As the leader of his army, Hayes was a figure that had played an important role in the success they'd had so far.

However, Hayes's army was outdated. His general status was obsolete. Eugene could sense Hayes trying to keep himself useful, despite his depleting uses. That was probably why Hayes was here – most people knew that Eugene liked to come and ogle at his creation, and Hayes was probably waiting for an attempt to bond over the thing Eugene loved most.

"Do you come up here often?" Eugene asked, trying to sense whether there was an ulterior motive to his presence.

"Occasionally. Just to watch them."

"They are quite something. Rather magnificent, if I do say so myself."

"They are."

"But I still believe we can do better."

Hayes stood.

"The day is approaching," Hayes said. "We are running out of time to create a whole new army."

Eugene smiled a smile that said he knew something, and he saw the look of concern on Hayes's face that he didn't know what this thing was.

"Oh, I know," Eugene said cockily. "Trust me, I know."

Eugene smoothed down the collar of his suit and made his way to the door.

"Care to walk with me?" he said, and Hayes obediently followed.

They made their way down the corridor, and down another, and down another, aimlessly wandering wherever their legs carried them.

Somehow, they ended up in the corridor Hayes often avoided, due to the constant sound of weeping. Eugene, however, enjoyed it. There was something about hearing a grown man cry that made him giddy.

They paused outside the room that contained the crying.

"Listen to that," Eugene said. "Just listen."

"Why don't you just put him out of his misery?" Hayes asked.

"Why ever would I do that?"

Eugene turned with a grin and peered through the narrow slit of glass.

There he sat, inside his square box, huddled in the corner.

Donny. The first subject to ever show substantial success in reacting to the new strand of infection.

"I will eventually," Eugene said. "But for now, he is our leverage. Gus Harvey and his gang of miscreants are the thorn in my side, and Donny is their weakness."

"But we have an army now," Hayes pointed out. Eugene noticed him abruptly retract, regretting his insolence.

"It doesn't hurt to have everything we can use." Eugene turned away from the door and they carried on walking. "Don't worry, as soon as we have no need for him, he will make a wonderful plate for the army's feast."

They carried on walking in content silence.

Chapter Sixteen

Gus awoke in the dead of night, his throat like a piece of sandpaper.

Maybe he was getting a cold. Or worse, flu. He could be getting ill.

But there was no time for illness in war. How many times did he or his friends have the flu in Afghanistan? They could hardly phone in sick, could they?

No, all he needed was some water. He'd left it in the kitchen.

He pushed himself off the sofa. He had no idea how he'd managed to fall asleep on the sofa in the first place, what with the loose springs and the dust clouds making him cough – but he'd endured worse. Far worse.

He made his way into the kitchen where he found Whizzo poking at something with a screwdriver. It looked like a box, with some random items attached that he couldn't make out in his tired state.

Gus bypassed him and went straight for the container, taking a few large swigs of water before dropping it with a satisfying "aah."

Then, he turned to Whizzo.

"Can't sleep?" Gus asked.

Whizzo shrugged.

"What's up?"

Whizzo stopped tampering with whatever he was tampering with and shoved it on the floor, then grabbed hold of the stump where his little finger used to be.

"Hurting?" Gus asked.

Whizzo nodded.

"Yeah, it does," Gus said, looking down at his own prosthetic leg – though, to be fair, the springs and movement of the leg Whizzo had made him were far better than the leg he'd had before.

"When does it stop?" Whizzo asked.

"Doesn't, really. Just get used to it. I mean, it stops killing, but it always feels a little uncomfortable."

"This is stupid."

"What?"

"No, not you. Just me, here, moaning about a missing finger, while you have a missing leg and you're walking around, not crying about it."

Gus chuckled.

"It sucks, either way," he said.

"Yeah, but I feel a bit pathetic."

Gus walked over to the table, pulled a chair out, and sat opposite Whizzo. The chairs were wooden; that uncomfortable kind of wooden that would grind against the bones of his buttocks, and he tried to shift into a more comfortable position.

"Listen," Gus said, taking another swig from the container then, noticing how little was left, putting the lid back on and placing it on the table. "You ain't pathetic. Far from it."

"I'm still a burden."

"A burden?"

"Yeah. I don't see you, Desert, or Sadie falling over and screwing up."

Gus leant back. Sighed. Considered Whizzo's words.

"What's this you're making?" Gus asked.

"Oh, it's nothing."

"Tell me."

Whizzo hesitated, looking over the box. There were a few explosives attached to it, which made Gus all the more intrigued.

"It's not even working. It's stupid."

"Just tell me."

Whizzo hesitated again.

"It's a bomb, but, not like a normal bomb."

Gus awaited further explanation, but when none came, he prompted further: "How so?"

"It traps water vapour inside. It contains loads of it, then when it goes off, it cools it quickly so that it becomes water. Because of the amount of water vapour it can trap, it then creates far more water than you could otherwise hold in the box."

"Wow. Sounds complicated."

"It sounds stupid. It's not even working. I just woke up and had this idea, and... Look at it. It's just a box with shit on the side."

Gus walked around the box. It was large, but not so big it wouldn't be impossible to transport.

"How would it even manage to do that?"

"Basically, I rigged it to have boiling water in one section, then water vapour in the other − done by creating a state of permanent condensation. Once the boiling liquid becomes pressurized liquid it will rupture its containment from the vapour, fall through it and expand the vapour into an explosion. I also have a small section of carbon dioxide that falls through like a bath bomb and it−"

"Whizzo, mate, I'm going to stop you right there." Gus chuckled. "None of this makes a bit of sense to me."

"Like I said, I don't know if this will even work, it's a stupid idea."

Gus leant forward.

"Yeah, but I tell you what – I'd never have thought about this idea. In fact, I wouldn't have even thought about where to start."

"That's because it's ridiculous."

"And the research you've been doing. Think I could make sense of that?"

"Probably."

"And this leg I have – think I'd have it if it weren't for you?"

Whizzo didn't answer.

"You couldn't be less of a burden. You've made these gadgets – and with nine fingers! It's just...you have your skillset, like I have mine."

"Yeah, but it's not a skillset that's helpful, is it? In a world like this you have to be able to fight and shoot guns, and I don't even know how to load one."

Gus shrugged.

"Could teach you if you like."

"We hardly have time. Do we?"

Gus sighed and stood. He considered saying more, but it didn't seem as if he was going to change Whizzo's mind.

"Good night, mate," he said instead.

Whizzo gave a half-hearted, unconvinced smile, and Gus returned to the living room for a few more hours of slumber.

BEFORE

Chapter Seventeen

Gus stumbled to his bed. The walls closed in on him like they always did, the claustrophobia melted his mind like it always had, and the room spun like his drunken mind always perceived.

There were many, many homes he could have chosen. Lavish mansions left vacated by dead millionaires, family homes left empty by deceased loved ones, or even other flats in the block that were slightly larger and just needed a bit of scrubbing to get the pieces of corpse off the wall.

But Gus deserved none of it.

No, this demented bedsit, stinking of his sick, the air tasting of booze – that was what he deserved.

And nothing more.

A man who lets his family down is nothing.

A man who kills his own family to save them from having to become feral, mindless creatures – who is that man?

What becomes of him?

This, he thought, rubbing his sinus. *This is what becomes of him.*

He took another swig from his whiskey bottle and scoffed at

what a cliché he'd become. From decorated veteran to alcoholic nomad. Even in the apocalypse there was still room for irony.

A few shrieks sounded from below.

He ignored them. He was used to the occasional sounds of death outside his window. He knew the other survivors wouldn't be survivors for long.

It meant nothing to him.

He wasn't a survivor. He was as much a victim as the dead.

He wandered around aimlessly, nothing to do, just eating when he could; no different than the infected.

"Help!" came a woman's cry from outside.

Help?

Who was she shouting to?

She couldn't know he was there. He never lit a candle, therefore there was no light to give him away -he preferred darkness, and his eyes had adjusted to it nicely.

"Please, somebody!"

Ah, well she was definitely not shouting to him.

He wasn't a *somebody*.

He was *nobody*.

"Oh my God, please, no!"

He huffed.

This was getting exasperating.

He placed his feet on the coarse frays of the carpet and stumbled, waving and shaking. He wiped the alcohol sweats from his brow and used the bed frame to steady himself.

He waited for the room to stop shaking, but that moment never came – so he waited for it to shake less. Once he had some coherence to his thoughts and stability in his sea legs, he meandered over to the window and peered out.

A woman, middle-aged, with a baby clutched to her chest, ran. Behind her, a man Gus assumed was her husband, wrestled one of the infected atop him.

"Just run!" the man shouted.

The woman went to run then didn't, pivoting, wanting to save her husband but wanting to protect her baby.

Gus could help.

But then what?

They'd run and make more noise – and with the incessant noise they were making, they were bound to be eaten at some point.

"Please!" she screamed.

He went to shut the curtains.

"Ron, no!"

He stopped.

The curtains remained half across the window, poised in his hands, matting beneath his rough skin.

Ron.

What was it about that name?

Ron.

"Ron, please! Somebody help!"

He remembered.

Ron was the name of the character.

The one he read to Laney.

He huffed. This was ridiculous. It was a fictional character, yet it pulled at his conscience enough to make him limp across the room and collect his gun.

He opened the window, took aim and fired.

The infected fell and Ron pushed it off, gaping at the hole in its head.

They looked up at him with tears of gratitude.

"Thank you!" the woman shouted. "Thank you so much!"

But it wasn't over.

Gus heard the rumble. The gunshot had attracted more of them. A horde was now approaching, and the tremble in the ground suggested there were a lot of them, and they were very close.

"Run!" Gus shouted.

Wanting to remain unnoticed by the horde, he shut the window and closed the curtains, returning to his bed.

The groans and heavy steps of the speeding horde passed outside.

He thought nothing more of the family.

He'd done his bit.

And he doubted they'd made it any further.

AFTER

Chapter Eighteen

The compound was both similar and different to what the facility had been. The facility was a number of buildings, whereas the compound was just one – yet it still took up the same vast amount of space. It was far from inconspicuous; in fact, it looked as official and domineering as a government building could, and the fence surrounding the perimeter did nothing to disguise its prominence.

Gus spotted the snipers atop the building first. They were going to be tricky to bypass. The snipers would, however, be looking for the infected rather than people – perhaps they could use that to their advantage.

They paused beside a set of trees, remaining low and out of sight.

"How should we do this?" Gus asked. Even though it was a general question aimed at the group, he looked at Desert, wanting to include her.

He couldn't help his glance still being wary, however – if they were to find Donny, he did not know what she was going to do.

"How many snipers do you think there are?" Desert said.

Gus tried to count, but there was no way to really know. They were in the distance, and they could only see the few that were visible on this side of the building.

"We can't be sure," he said.

"Maybe if we create a distraction, and the rest of us–"

"Guys," Whizzo interrupted, unravelling a few pieces of paper and looking over them.

"What?" Gus said

"I'm pretty sure there's an underground entrance." Whizzo eventually found the diagram he needed. "Yeah, on the north side."

Gus raised his arm to create a shadow from the sun, which he used to deduce that the north side was to their right.

"Let's find out," he said and, remaining crouched, stepped as lightly as his boots would allow him through the wooded area.

They found one of the infected staring gormlessly at a tree. Gus raised a hand to pause the others, withdrew his hunting knife, ran up behind it and slid the knife into the base of its skull.

They continued around and, sure enough, they found it. A door beneath a sloping roof leading into the ground. Two guards stood outside.

Desert went to aim her gun, but Gus gave a stern headshake.

"You don't want to kill them?" she snapped.

"I don't want to attract a horde," Gus replied in a shouting whisper.

She nodded and withdrew her knife.

Instinctively, Gus knew to take the person on the right, which meant he had to get to the other side of them unnoticed. He remained as low as he could, practically on his belly, and shuffled past the bushes and around the trees until he was out of sight, yet close enough to introduce an element of surprise.

He searched out Desert and saw her hiding in a similar position to the left of the guards. Gus lifted three fingers on his hand, counted down to two, then to one, then with a nod of their heads they rushed out.

The guards went to aim their guns but weren't afforded the time to shoot. Gus grabbed the end of his man's gun, tilted it so the trigger could not be fired, and swung his knife into the man's neck. The man gurgled blood, but Gus couldn't be sure this was enough, and he couldn't risk this guy firing his gun and attracting unwanted attention – so he slid out the knife and jabbed the man in the gut a few times.

Once he was able to take the man's gun from him, Gus let the guard drop to the floor, where he spluttered the last moments of his life. He turned to his left and found Desert's guy doing the same.

They threw the guns into a nearby bush – they already had guns and didn't want to carry anything else. A quick search of the bodies revealed a set of keys, and Gus used them to unlock the door.

The corridor was painted solely in darkness. Desert and Gus took out their guns and entered, followed by Sadie and Whizzo. Their steps echoed, and they moved slowly and cautiously.

Whizzo took two flashlights from his bag and handed them to Desert and Gus, who fixed them to their guns.

"What would I do without you, kid?" Gus whispered.

The light didn't do much to illuminate their way, but it at least gave them reassurance that nothing was coming toward them.

The corridor began to rise, and they found themselves walking upwards. They reached a set of steps that led to a light, and it was at this moment that Gus and Desert exchanged a glance and killed their lights.

Keeping their guns aimed, they ascended toward the light, which appeared through the window of a door. As they approached, the view through the window began to gain clarity.

Yet they didn't quite conceive the view.

It didn't seem real.

Gus shook his head, trying to break the hallucination.

But it wasn't a hallucination.

What they could see was real, and it changed everything.

Chapter Nineteen

G us had presumed that he would find some more research.

A few test subjects, maybe.

At worse, a handful similar to Donny but not quite as strong yet.

Not this.

Never this.

"What the fuck is this?" Desert asked, the only one of them able to talk.

Whizzo tried to speak, feeling that he was the one who should give the answer – but all that fell from his mouth were stuttering syllables.

Even Sadie withdrew a little. Gus felt her hand grip around his arm as her body recoiled back.

They were masses of them. And they weren't just higher functioning specimens waiting around – they were training. Working hard to increase their abilities even further.

There was still something about them that was off... Still something zombie-like... With enough human about them to think, but enough inhuman to obey the handlers.

Just imagine what kinds of things those handlers could ask them to do...

Gus shook his head. Tried to snap himself out of it. His eyes were mistaken. They had to be. This was not what he expected.

But it was what was there.

"Whizzo," he grunted, once he was able to find his voice again. "Is this what you were expecting?"

"Er... No... And yes, I guess... But mainly, no."

"What do you mean?"

"I knew there were designs to create something like this, I skimmed over them, but I – I never thought..." He sighed, rubbing his hands over his face. "I think we should go back. Let me look at the rest of the research and I can try to figure out what these things are."

"Go back?" Desert said. "We can't just... This is..."

Gus put a hand on her shoulder. A move he didn't think was wise but suddenly felt bold enough to do.

"I know," he said. "We can't allow this, can't leave it, we have to do something – but I don't think now is the time. Look at them, look at us."

Desert nodded. She seemed to agree.

Yet, Gus didn't turn to go.

What could these things be capable of?

And why would anyone want to create them?

What was Eugene Squire planning?

All of these questions and more were hanging in the air, unanswered.

Is this what the infection was actually meant for?

Then he looked to Sadie.

He recalled the experimentation and torture she endured when they were contained within the facility.

And he realised.

I led her right to them...

Without Sadie, this couldn't have happened. Sadie's genes

had a partial resistance to the infection that they had been able to utilise.

It was her blood that began this creation.

It was Donny who was the test subject.

And Gus had brought Sadie to their facility, led her right into their hands.

He loved Sadie, but he decided that, for the sake of the world's future – he would have been better off leaving her where they found her.

Sadie looked questioningly at him. He realised he was staring at her.

He rested his palm on the side of her cheek and she bowed her head into it.

No. He couldn't blame him or her for what bad men had done.

Either way, it was time to go.

"Come on," Gus instructed.

He gave a final glance at the mass of superior infected.

Was Donny among them?

He scanned every body and every face, but there was no sign.

He wanted to jump down and search every one of them more thoroughly, but he had to heed his own advice – now was not the time.

He led them back to the corridor that led them back underground. Within seconds they had re-entered the darkness.

He didn't bother with the flashlight.

It was straight tunnel to the other side, and he'd hear any infected approaching.

Though, to be honest, the regular infected were now the least of his worries.

He checked behind himself and he could hear the tapping of the others' feet. There was no conversation, no talking, no verbal engagement – just wary steps.

Everyone seemed to be stepping a lot lighter than they had on the way there.

But there was some heavier tapping. Some footsteps he didn't recognise.

Which one of them was that?

But the heavier tapping was not coming from behind him.

"Stop," Gus whispered, halting, the others doing the same

He listened.

There it was.

Heavy steps. A few of them.

Lights came on through the corridor. So bright, Gus had to turn his head away and shield his eyes.

Once he had readjusted, he looked up and there they were.

Eugene Squire with that same smug look on his privileged, arrogant face.

General Boris Hayes on one side.

Donny on the other.

Though Donny was not standing tall and proud like the others.

He was on a lead. In rags. Crouched on the floor. Cowering and snarling. Eugene Squire's bitch.

Chapter Twenty

"Donny..." Gus muttered in a voice so weak he didn't recognise it as his own.

"I know," said Eugene, that same smackable grin plastered cleanly across his pale face. "I know, I know. I take it you saw them?"

Gus looked over his shoulder at the others.

They said nothing.

"Let him go," Gus demanded.

"Oh, are you sure you really want me to do that? He's quite feisty when he's off his lead! Doesn't play well with others."

Gus felt his nails digging into his palm.

Whizzo had backed away, Desert had taken out her gun, and Sadie was bursting to get at Eugene – and it took all the strength in Gus's arm to stop her.

"I," Gus began, taking a step toward Eugene, "am going to kill you."

"Are you?" Eugene replied, sticking his bottom lip out.

"It may not be today. It may not be tomorrow. But I swear it."

"Yes, yes, rather. Anyway. Enough of empty threats. Let's play."

Eugene clicked a button on Donny's collar and Donny pounced without any hesitation. He jumped on Gus, retracted his arm and threw a heavy fist full-on into Gus's face.

A crack echoed, and Gus was pretty sure it was his nose.

He braced himself for another, but it didn't come.

That was because Donny had seen the gun Desert was aiming at him.

"Don't shoot!" Gus said, but it made no difference. Desert hadn't a chance to put any pressure on the trigger before Donny had leapt forward and stolen the gun from her hands.

Donny hit the butt of it into Desert's face and she stumbled back.

He hit her again and she fell to the floor.

He hit her again.

And again.

And again.

He was like beast uncaged. A wild animal let loose of its restraints, intent on carnage. The human element of Donny had gone, and he was a savage predator.

Eugene's laughter combined with the sound of pummelling.

Gus dove at Donny, but Donny leapt out of the way and Gus ended up on top of Desert. She was groggy, and some of her blood made it onto Gus's arm.

Donny thrust forward at Whizzo, speedily on all fours. Whizzo ran, then remembered what he was running toward if he carried on down the corridor.

He paused, poised between coming and going, and closed his eyes as if making peace with his demise.

Gus, getting more incensed by the constant laughter – *hoh, hoh, hoh* – did his best to ignore it and ran at Donny. He managed to tackle Donny before a third strike could be landed into Whizzo's face.

Donny turned back on Gus.

"Sadie!" Gus cried. "Help!"

Sadie looked the most distraught of all of them. She was crying, wanting to help Gus but not wanting to harm Donny – caught between two choices she didn't want to choose.

In the end, she curled into a ball and buried her head in her arms.

There was nothing Gus could do but accept the inevitable beating.

Donny's fists rained down on him from cheek to cheek. Both of his arms were going; as soon as one was in the air, the other landed.

Then he uncurled his fists and used his hands instead. His dirty nails scratched at Gus, pulling skin off his face and ripping his cheeks to raggedy streaks of red.

"Donny!" Gus cried out, fighting the agony, fighting the pain.

There was no stopping him. Donny was relentless.

"Donny, stop!"

Donny lifted his hand into the air.

Readied the nails.

Looked down at Gus's throat.

This is it.

The end.

The full stop.

The final curtain.

"What're you going to do, Donny? Kill me?"

Donny's eyes glowered red and Eugene could be seen over his shoulder, hands clasped together with excitement.

"What, you going to kill me like you did Janine Stanton?"

Donny's face flickered with raw emotion.

His hand didn't descend to Gus.

It remained poised.

Hovering.

Stuck in mid-air.

Gus saw the real Donny behind those eyes.

And he took his chance.

He pushed Donny off, grabbed the gun from Desert's side and pointed it at Hayes, who pointed a gun back.

"Back off," Gus demanded.

Hayes did not back off, but he did not fire.

"Get up," Gus urged Desert. She pushed herself to her feet, staring at the blood landing in small puddles beneath her.

"Come on," he said, and he walked past Hayes, their guns still aimed at one another's heads.

Whizzo walked past with his arm around Desert, who limped and clutched her eye.

Sadie remained next to Donny, who was dormant on the floor, perturbed, somehow broken.

"We'll come back for him," Gus told her. "Come on."

Reluctantly, she moved, and followed the others.

To Gus's surprised, Hayes lowered his weapon.

Instead, Hayes took out a small gadget, with a button.

He pressed the button.

An alarm pierced Gus's head and his forehead throbbed, feeling as if his brain was going to expand and burst against his skull.

A mass of footsteps came running.

Entering the corridor.

Coming closer.

Gus didn't have to ask what that was.

"Run," he said.

"What?" Whizzo asked, his face changing as he realised what was coming.

Desert looked weakly up at Gus.

"Run!" he shouted.

And he ran.

Sadie at his side.

Whizzo and Desert following. Desert struggling, then looking back at the oncoming faces and forcing herself to move.

Adrenaline powered them to the end of the corridor and they emerged into the forest, where they kept running.

It took seconds for the army to appear behind them.

Chapter Twenty-One

In a way, Gus came to accept that all of them were probably not going to make it.

Then he scolded himself for accepting it.

He ran ahead with Sadie at his side. A glance over his shoulder told him that Desert still had enough about her that she could run with Whizzo encouraging her.

But, behind Desert and Whizzo, there they were.

Catching up, and catching up quickly.

"To the lake!"

The sight of them in the light and in attack mode was something to behold. Gus didn't have time to stop and look, but he had enough of a glance to see what terrifying creatures had been created. They were like the infected, but with skin more ripped than pale and dead. They were still unaware, relying on instinct, yes – but there was enough about them to obey instructions. The stench of death they carried was stronger, their steps heavier, and their faces just as aggressively eager to feed on their prey.

Gus reached the nearby lake and paused for the others.

Sadie backed away from the lake, refusing to go in. Gus took her hand and said, "It's okay, get on my back."

He helped her up, but she was still shaking, terrified of the water.

Desert dove in and Whizzo followed. They swam, though they didn't swim fast.

Gus ran into the water, feeling a set of outstretched fingers skim his remaining leg.

Once the water was up to his shoulders, Sadie clinging so tightly that he struggled to breathe, he turned back and looked at them.

Paused.

They had stopped, paces away, refusing to even make contact with the water's edge.

Masses of them lined the fluid barrier, reaching their hands out but unable to get him in their grasp.

Their teeth snapped.

Eyes opened.

Saliva drooled out of snarling mouths.

They were lucky.

So god damn lucky.

If this lake hadn't been so close...

Sadie whimpered into Gus's ear and he stroked her arm.

"It's okay, I got you," he said.

He gave the army one more look, accompanied by his middle finger, then turned.

He swam away, weighed down by Sadie but just able to remain afloat.

He saw Whizzo ahead, struggling to keep Desert above water. As he approached, he could see that she'd passed out.

Gus lifted Desert's hand and gave it to Sadie.

"Hold this," he instructed.

She took it, Desert's arm shaking under Sadie's tremble. Whizzo took the other arm and, in a very slow swim, they carried on. It took a while, but they reached the other side of the lake.

Once Sadie had released Gus's throat and Desert had been laid upon the wet grass, Gus felt for her pulse. Her face was mangled, her nose twisted and both eyes blackened – but she was alive.

"She's fine," he reassured Whizzo.

Whizzo nodded, though he looked a little angry.

He knew what Whizzo was thinking.

If Desert had shot that gun before you stopped her, she'd be fine right now.

There was no way to know that, but he understood.

If the situation was reversed and the same thing had happened to Sadie, he would not be forgiving.

"Let's just get her back."

He took Sadie over his shoulder and they carried on walking.

BEFORE

Chapter Twenty-Two

With a hobble and a grimace, Gus stomped down the open street. Dust scattered across his face and the smell of decay hung on the air like a child clinging to its favourite toy.

There were no infected around. Not as far as Gus could see, anyway – and not that he'd care; he'd happily be killed and eaten and be able to end his misery.

Yet, despite the lack of undead, their smell still remained. It's what everything smelt of now. Every street, every looted shop and every burnt-out village. The ashes that floated across the wind no longer smelt like the fire that had created their decay.

Even he stank of it. His clothes, his hair, his skin. He hadn't washed in weeks and the repulsive smell had replaced his body odour in becoming his natural scent.

He kicked open the door to the supermarket. It was somehow jammed, skewwhiff and bent from its hinges. He gave a harder nudge with his shoulder and it opened. The annoying ding of the store bell announced his entry.

There was little left. The remnants of the store were strewn across empty shelves and stained floors. The occasional spot of blood or wayward limb marked his path, but he ignored it. Blood and limbs were as normal as bread and butter to both him, and the world he now inhabited.

And it didn't matter that there was little food left.

His stomach gurgled and spluttered, but he didn't care about his hunger. He'd been hungry for a while and he was used to it. His skin clung to his ribs and his beefy arms looked unnatural next to them, but with a bullet lodged in his leg, he'd always he safe in the knowledge that there would never be any other part of his body as fucked up as his calf.

He limped past the magazines, the empty vegetable crates and the ransacked pharmaceuticals.

He arrived at an aisle with a large sign above it reading *13 Beer / Wine.*

There was still enough left. It seemed that people had prioritised scavenging food rather than such necessities as booze.

He grabbed a basket and hobbled over to the wines. He'd never been able to afford the really, really expensive wines, but here they were. Free for the taking.

He picked a bottle of vintage red and unscrewed the top. He lifted his head back and took more large gulps than his body could handle, and faster than his throat could accommodate.

Damn, that's good shit.

He grabbed the rest of the bottles and shoved them in the basket, holding the open bottle in his other hand, and taking further swigs as he made his way to the spirits.

A few bottles of whiskey had collapsed over one another. He didn't even bother looking at the brand. It was whiskey, which meant it would all be good. He shoved them into the basket.

The basket was growing heavy, but there was still room. He grabbed a few bottles of amber ale and limped away.

He had what he came for.

He went back past the pharmaceuticals, past the empty vegetable crates, and past the magazines.

He paused.

Even some of the television magazines were missing.

Who would want an out of date television magazine?

He dropped the basket and meandered down the aisle. Past the women's monthlies and men's health magazines and something about metal music and then the books.

And there it was.

In the middle of a shelf, nothing else around it.

The final copy.

A new cover, not like the one he used to have.

The Ever-present.

He didn't know whether to cry or snap *fuck you* at the book.

He did neither.

Just stared.

It was like the book was taunting him. Like it had been placed there deliberately, knowingly.

There were no other books around it. The rest of the shelves had ripped, blood-splattered books strewn haphazardly over one another.

Not this shelf.

No, not this shelf.

This shelf had this one book. There. Ready. Waiting for him.

Should he take it?

What then?

He screamed. Punched his fist into another shelf, the books clattering to the floor, his knuckles flaking dead skin.

But he didn't punch the shelf with this book on.

He crouched. Covered his face. He refused to fall to his knees, but he had to lower himself somehow, had to collapse into his grief.

He grabbed the book and charged back to his basket, put it between two bottles of wine, and left.

AFTER

Chapter Twenty-Three

Gus awoke with his arm around Sadie. He hadn't fallen asleep that way, nor had Sadie been anywhere near him when his eyes had closed – but there she was. Beneath his arm, asleep, and soundly so.

It was strange how much she desired not just attention, but affection. Like a pet, like something that...

Gus's eyes opened.

Alert.

That's it...

A sudden realisation sparked something in his mind, a realisation that was so obvious he couldn't believe it hadn't occurred to him yet. In fact, he couldn't believe it hadn't occurred to Whizzo yet.

But no, it couldn't be that simple.

Could it?

He thought back to his confrontation with Donny from a few days ago – a confrontation that had prompted Desert to cease all talking to him whatsoever, going from spiteful glances to no glances at all.

What had stopped Donny from killing him?

It was a mention of Doctor Janine Stanton...

The doctor who did this to him...

But maybe there was more to it than that...

Maybe he and Stanton had become closer. Maybe she'd had been nicer toward him. Maybe she was reluctant to administer the treatment she had been forced into...

He gently moved Sadie off and placed her down. She groaned gently, but didn't stir.

He rushed into the kitchen where Whizzo sat at the table with his research, and Desert sat over a can of something she was scooping out with a rusty spoon.

She still looked groggy. Beaten. Her eyes were no longer just black, but blacky blue. Her cheek had a scab going all the way up to her eye, and her eyelids still flickered with a distant pain.

"I have it," Gus announced.

Whizzo looked up. Desert didn't.

"Have what?" Whizzo asked. He looked tired, and his question seemed impatient.

"How we can save Donny."

Desert scoffed. The closest thing to an interaction they'd had in a while.

Even Whizzo sighed, rested his head on his hand and closed his eyes for a moment, as if to think, *are we really doing this again?*

"Look, I know you're sceptical, and you have every right to be, but I really think I'm onto something."

"Look, Gus..." Whizzo began, then trailed off.

Gus knew what they were thinking.

They thought that Gus was so adamant, so stubborn, that he was bordering on delusional.

He knew, because he'd think the same thing.

But he honestly thought he had it.

"Just listen to me," Gus urged them, and felt a little angry about it. He'd never had to justify himself to anyone before.

"Fine," Whizzo said, leaning back and lifting his arms in the air. Desert shook her head. "What is it?"

"Emotions!" Gus said, then left it hanging there as if it explained something.

Whizzo returned Gus's look expectantly, requiring further explanation.

"Right, look at Sadie," Gus continued. "She has the infection, we know that. She has it on a different level, but it's still the same thing *they* have. Yet, look at her – I wake up most nights with her cuddled up to me. She refused to even fight Donny because she cared too much for him."

Whizzo nodded, then waited for Gus to continue.

"Then take Donny the other day – he almost killed me. Then I mentioned the name Doctor Janine Stanton, the doctor who administered his infection, who Donny would have some kind of, I don't know, emotional connection to."

Gus paused again, prompting Whizzo to say, "And?"

"Don't you see? They are displaying human emotions. That is how we get him back!"

Desert stopped eating and slammed her fists on the table. She tried to remain still but her leg was shaking.

"I think we're past the point of getting him back," Whizzo said. "Don't you?"

"Look, I know how this must sound, and I ain't asking permission, I'm, I don't know – asking for help. I think we can save him, I honestly do, we–"

Desert stood, took her can of food, and threw it across the room.

"Fuck off!" she shouted, her voice straining under the volume. Gus instinctively went to tell her to be quiet as she may attract the infected, then decided not to.

She stared at Gus, who stared back.

"Look at me!" she asserted. "Look at me! *He* did this. *Donny* did this. He isn't your mate anymore, he isn't something we can save."

"I understand why you–"

"No you don't."

"Do not interrupt me!" Gus screamed, slamming his fist so hard into the wall it left a round dent and dust scattered.

Desert looked horrified.

"Who are you?" Gus said. "Who the fuck are you? What, just over a year ago you were some secretary and you turned badass and now you think you know all about this?"

"And you do?"

"I served! I fought, I killed, I watched friends die and enemies win, and I did it for years! So don't *fuck* with me!"

An uncomfortable silence hung as the eye of the storm passed. Then the storm resumed.

"I know what he did to you," Gus continued, his voice low but still menacing. "I can see it, and I bet it hurt like hell. He pummelled me too, almost killed me in fact. But you don't know shit. You're angry, and you don't know shit."

"So what," Desert said, "you're just going to appeal to his better side and he'll stop? Pull on his heart strings? Make him cry?"

"Desert–" Whizzo tried, but was ignored.

"Who else does he need to kill until you get a fucking grip?"

Gus stepped closer to her. "Everyone," he answered. He looked to Whizzo. "Surely you think it could work?"

Whizzo shrugged. "Even if there was some element of human emotion still there, I don't know how we'd utilise it to stop him."

"Then we figure it out," Gus said. "Right? We figure it out."

"Tell you what," Desert interjected. "If you get one of those zombies wandering around outside, and you find their human-ity, I'll go along with you. You get one of them to sing you a hymn or watch Titanic with you, and tell them not to kill you, and they don't, then I'll go with you. Otherwise..."

Gus knew she was being sarcastic, but he didn't care.

"Fine," Gus said.

Desert scoffed.

"Fine," she said.

She marched into the other room.

"Gus–" Whizzo went to say.

"No," Gus interrupted. "Don't say anything. I got to go catch me a zombie."

He pushed the rusty fridge away from the wall, grabbed the wire from behind it, and pulled it off. Flexing it and checking its length, he picked up his blade and exited the house.

Chapter Twenty-Four

Gus muttered to himself in grunts and inaudible sentences as he stumbled down the steep slope from the run-down house and further into the forest. It took minutes until he was surrounded by trees and branches obscured the sun.

If he really thought about it, he could understand Desert's point of view – he could understand it all too well. To take a beating like that, watch her friend die and not wish vengeance would be inhuman. If she wasn't angry and refusing to give in to Gus's determination to find some of the old Donny still left in him, then one would have to wonder what was wrong with her.

But Gus didn't really think about it.

He refused to acknowledge that she may have a point.

He knew his perspective was obscured and he was okay with that.

He would not let Donny down.

And if that cost them more than just their lives? If that cost them the ability to stop this army achieving whatever it was Eugene planned to achieve with them?

Then fuck it.

Donny went back for him. And he didn't have to, but he did. Gus was taken by a cannibalistic family and Donny took a gun, shaking in his hands, and fired it, overcoming a fear that had impaled his ability to defend himself for so long.

Most importantly, Donny taught Gus how to care about someone other than himself again.

He had taught Gus that there was reason to live.

His muttering ceased as he heard a groan come closer.

He readied his knife, flexing his fingers over the leather handle.

He paused.

Listened.

The groans grew louder.

The steps grew quicker.

It had seen him. Wherever it was coming from, it was running, and it was quickly approaching.

He'd seen how they could run. How quick they were. He had to be alert.

But which direction were they coming from?

He closed his eyes. Listened even more intently.

He opened his eyes and turned to his right.

Legs apart. Arms by his side. Eyes wide open, mind alert.

Ready.

He saw it. Approaching from behind the trees. Bumping into the odd stump, a twig attached to its foot. By the look of it, it was once a man. Probably had blond hair, though that was a guess as it was now thick with mud. It wore a raggedy t-shirt, red, ripped, a Manchester United emblem still attached.

Gus had despised Manchester United.

Strange, how such trivial hatred seemed so important at the time.

Its eyes opened wider as it saw what it had heard and smelt.

It had a limp as well. Something Gus could relate to.

Just as it reached him with outstretched arms, Gus fell to

the floor and swiped his blade through the base of its right knee. Its leg detached and the infected collapsed.

He mounted its back and stretched the cable he'd taken from the back of the fridge around its neck.

Before it could find its way to its one good foot, Gus began walking, clutching the cable, dragging it behind him. It took all of his strength to take the body up the hill. He'd always imagined one of the infected would be lighter, which was odd, as a corpse was usually quite heavy.

He reached the door to the house and took the cable in one hand and the infected's hair in the other. He used his buttocks to push down on the door handle and back his way into the house.

Whizzo looked up, did a double take, then leapt from his seat and backed up against the wall.

"Woah!" he shouted. "What the hell are you doing?"

Gus dragged the infected through the kitchen.

Desert appeared at the doorway. She became instantly alert and withdrew her gun.

"What the fuck!" she said.

"Don't shoot it!" Gus urged her.

"What, we're saving the regular infected now as well?"

Gus held its head away from his, and looked down at the snapping jaw doing all it could to get to him.

Sadie appeared in the doorway and instantly went to attack.

"No, don't!" Gus said, putting out a hand to signal halt.

"Are you completely out of your fucking mind?" Desert demanded.

"You said it, didn't you?" Gus said.

"What?"

"That if I could find one of the infected and get them not to kill me, that you'd go along with saving Donny."

"I didn't seriously think you'd do that!"

"Well here it is. Where's the basement?"

"The basement? Are you seriously going to make us sleep above this thing!"

"It'll be tied up, relax."

Desert still looked at him with an intense glare of *you are crazy*.

"Just get out of my way," Gus demanded, fed up.

He dragged the infected to a doorway that he presumed led to the basement. The infected snarled as it bumped down the steps.

Gus found a pipe running across the ceiling and he attached the other side of the cable to it with numerous swift knots.

He made his way back up the steps and, once he'd shut the door behind him, looked for a way to lock it. Without a lock, he grabbed a chair from the kitchen and propped it against the handle.

"You are seriously fucked up," Desert said. "So is this."

"I will not leave this door," Gus said. "I will guard it day and night. You don't need to worry."

"But you–"

"Look – you told me if I could get one of the infected and appeal to some kind of emotion, you'd help save Donny, yeah?"

"Yeah, but I never thought you'd actually–"

"Well I have. So get over it. And give it this one chance. Okay?"

Desert backed down, but still solemnly shook her head, as if pitying a helpless idiot.

"I still think this is stupid."

"Like I give a shit."

Gus barged past her and into the kitchen, searching out some water. Catching this thing had been thirsty work and he didn't want to spend another minute with Desert.

Not because she was wrong.

Because she was right.

Chapter Twenty-Five

Donny leant his head against the hard softness of the padded wall.

Are you going to kill me like you did Janine Stanton?

He hadn't killed her.

It was a lie.

The girl had.

Hadn't she?

In all honesty, he wasn't even sure who he had killed.

He felt bad about it. There was something resembling a conscience, though it was musky and blurred and faraway.

An abrupt itch on his neck made him scratch at his collar.

Why didn't he take it off?

I can't.

Why did he attack those people?

Because I must.

Where was Janine Stanton?

I should hate her.

He should.

Stanton injected him. Pushed needles into his skin and wrote stuff on paper and clipboards and watched him as he writhed and hurt and she always watched and wrote and watched and wrote and watched and wrote and–

But she wasn't like the others.

Not like Eugene who petted him but it wasn't a nice pet it was patronising like something he shouldn't be doing but he did and Donny let him because...

Because...

I must.

It was his reason, his cause, and his excuse.

But Stanton...

She pushed that stuff into him and watched him change but she never petted him. She never patronised him.

In fact, she spoke to him.

No one ever spoke to him. Not unless it was a command, or an instruction, or some kind of experiment or game like they did when they were teaching him how to...

How to what?

But Janine.

She was nice. She never seemed willing to do those horrible things she did to him and he loved her for it.

He had to cooperate.

Why?

Because I must.

He was strapped to a chair but that meant nothing.

He'd never hurt her.

Or would he?

Are you going to kill me like you did Janine Stanton?

Did he kill her?

Did he do it because he must?

He didn't want to.

It was the aggression, the desire to feed, to hurt, to find a way to peel away their skin and graze on what was beneath.

I must.

I must.

I must I must I must I must I must.

Janine Stanton was a kind woman. She spoke to him.

He never replied, but she still spoke.

They had full conversations he was never part of.

He had watched her die.

Had he done it?

I must.

Wait, what?

He must what?

Footsteps passed the door and he leapt to his feet but they kept on walking and eventually they stopped.

They left.

Like everyone leaves.

I must.

Must what?

Hurt?

Kill?

Feed?

He collapsed onto his back. The ceiling was spinning. The padding was uncomfortable on his spine.

I must.

That's right, Donny.

You must.

Now there's a good boy.

Chapter Twenty-Six

With a few clumsy knocks and bangs Gus managed to get the kitchen chair through the narrow doorway to the basement. He hoisted it over his shoulder and began his descent, wondering if the infected was at all dormant – but the snarls and yaps had already intensified before his prosthetic limb even met the second step.

The zombie pulled and dragged and heaved and tugged on the restraint fixed around its throat, opening and closing its jaw, desperate to be fed.

Gus wretched as he reached the bottom step. The stench of decay and rot met him like a sucker-punch to the gut. The stink seemed to have attached itself to every part of the room. It clung to the walls, mixing with the damp, sullying the air. Even his clothes seemed to stink of it.

He placed his chair beneath the light – a single bulb gently illuminating the room and casting the walls and corners in shadow.

The infected did not give in. It reached out its arms and pulled on the cable with as much vigour and strength as it could muster. Gus thought he saw the drainpipe give a little, and wondered if their superior strength might be too much for this weak house – but something seemed to be making it slower. Starvation, possibly. He had no idea how many survivors were even left; for all he knew, it could have been out there a long time without feeding.

Gus withdrew his knife and held it in the air.

"I'm putting this down," he said.

The infected didn't even look at the knife. It reached desperately for Gus.

Nevertheless, Gus placed the knife on the floor behind him.

"I'm doing this to show you that I am unarmed," he continued. "And that there is trust here."

He stood and lifted his top, turning in a full circle, then lifted his left trouser leg to expose a naked ankle.

"And you can see there are no guns on me. I am completely unarmed. Because there is trust."

The infected couldn't give less of a shit.

It didn't seem to understand a word – and, what's more, it didn't seem to care. Its pulling and snapping and reaching just continued with the same enthusiasm it had since Gus had entered the basement.

"Right," Gus decided. "Shall we begin?"

He pulled a book from his back pocket.

He ran his thumb over the cover. Flicked the browned pages and coughed on puffs of dust.

"I'm going to read you some of this book," Gus said. "I have no idea what happens in it, but it's my favourite book."

He sighed.

This was already taking a lot from him, and he'd barely started.

"The Ever-present," Gus announced, showing the infected the title.

Already, he was wiping his eyes on his sleeve, fighting an image of Laney snuggled up to him, her eyes slowly closing then suddenly opening as she adamantly stayed awake. He could still smell the shampoo from her bath, could still feel her small hands resting on the rough skin of his palm, could still hear her insistence that they kept going.

He huffed. Composed himself. Opened to the first page.

"It was a tough day," he began. "But it was never tough enough for Roy."

He stopped.

He dropped the book to his knees.

Maybe he should find another?

No. This is the book that meant the most to me.

He had to show emotion. Had to display those thoughts and feelings he had buried behind his spiralling thoughts.

"He could take a cast-iron morning," he began again, forcing confidence to his voice, "and turn it into a fluffy afternoon."

He ignored another image of Laney, begging him not to stop, begging for just another page.

"His hands were rough from working, and his belly hard from drinking, but underneath, his soul was as elegant and beautiful as a soul ever could be."

He looked up at the infected.

Nothing had changed.

Its eyes were wide, dilating at the sight of meat.

It pulled and stretched and grasped and snatched.

Gus ignored it.

"He worked hard, day and night," he persevered. "Tooth and nail, as his old man would say – though his teeth were sparse and his nails broken."

Please, Daddy, just one more page...

"Still, he worked tooth and nail, as it is said, until he had enough to provide his child with central heating and a puppy and..."

Don't stop, Daddy.

"...every other pleasure..."

Please go away.

"...he could dote upon them."

He dropped the book. Stood and kicked the chair across the room.

The infected reached for him.

He stood closer. Close enough that the stale fingers of the dead could brush against his collar.

"You don't feel anything, do you?"

No let up.

No rest.

No pause in its hunger.

He grabbed the book and stuffed it into his back pocket.

"This is so stupid," he told himself, and marched up the stairs.

Chapter Twenty-Seven

A s soon as Eugene received the call, he was out of his office and down the corridor with a haste his legs could barely keep up with.

He felt giddy.

Like a child.

Shaking with glee.

By the time he'd reached the laboratory he was practically bouncing. He paused, willed himself to calm down, told himself that he still had an image to portray and he would not command respect if he acted like an excitable schoolboy.

Not that he commanded respect, anyway.

But that was about to change.

He smoothed down his collar, straightened his tie, and entered, slowly and particularly, looking around and enjoying the hush that descended over the room upon his appearance.

Doctor Charles Moore saw Eugene and sighed, keeping his hesitation inside.

Eugene ignored the subordination. This was too good a day.

"Well?" Eugene prompted. "I'm here. Where is it?"

"This way," Charles reluctantly answered.

He led Eugene across the laboratory and to a microscope.

"What the bloody hell is this? Where is it?"

"Please, look."

Eugene looked through the microscope.

He saw something that even his unscientific yet twisted, ambitious mind understood. Splodges of red blood cells swam around until they were helplessly engulfed by larger splodges, turning a darker red, then throbbing and convulsing. When the petri dish smashed, Eugene jumped back and clapped.

"Marvellous!" he said. "Just marvellous!"

"I'm glad you're pleased with it," Charles said insincerely.

"And have you created a synthesis?"

Charles nodded and led Eugene over to his desk. There, on the desk, sat a needle, prominent yet unassuming. Full of a dark greenish red substance, ready and waiting for use.

"Do you have more?"

"No, this is the only one."

"Good. I don't want you to produce anymore."

"What?" Charles's mouth fell agape. He thought Eugene wanted to enhance his army – why would he not want more?

Was all of this work for nothing?

Eugene grinned at Charles's confusion.

"I would like you to destroy all notes, all research, all samples, aside from this one here."

"But – but why?"

"You hated creating this, didn't you? I could tell. Yet now you are fond of it?"

"It's just... the work that has gone into it..."

Eugene ignored the pathetic cries of a grown man and lifted the needle, holding it before his eyes, marvelling at it. The liquid inside did not stay still – it thrashed and pushed against its plastic containment. It was practically alive already, without even needing a host.

"Tell me," Eugene said. "How is this better than the gene we already have?"

"Oh, it's better all right," Charles said. "There's more of the infection in it, but it's more controlled – we have managed to pull out elements of the gene and neglect some others. The strength, the speed, the hostility – it's all been enhanced. The mindless wandering is gone, but you will need to bear in mind that may affect the obedience."

"That's fine. There doesn't need to be any obedience."

Charles frowned. Eugene waited for him to muster up the courage to say what was on his mind, so much so Eugene grew irritable and had to prompt him.

"Say it," Eugene commanded. "What?"

"It's just – if you don't mind my asking, sir – why did you want us to work so hard on it if you only want one sample?"

Eugene's grin widened, turning all the more intensely lecherous.

He stuck the needle into his arm and plunged down slightly.

"How much do I need?" Eugene asked.

"Erm, that much should have the effect, any more would–"

Eugene cut Charles off by pushing down upon the injection until all of the substance had entered his body. He took the empty needle out and discarded it.

He closed his eyes.

Waited for it.

"How long should it take?" Eugene demanded.

"Erm, well, the infection usually takes minutes, if that."

Eugene nodded.

Minutes weren't needed.

He could already feel it. A grand dizziness. A superior headrush.

He collapsed to his knees. Bent over. Hunched. Shaking.

He spat blood, spraying it over the clean, hard surface of the floor.

He wobbled, falling onto his back, convulsing, until he was

seizing, foam bubbling out his mouth.

No one did anything.

Charles watched abhorrently.

It wasn't like anyone wanted to save him. No one shouted for a medic, or first aid. No one attempted to administer it. This was Eugene's own stupid fault.

The seizure stopped.

Eugene lay there, his eyes wide open yet unmoving, staring at the ceiling. Dormant. Frozen. Stiff.

"Mr Squire?" Charles asked, then looked to his approaching colleagues, a smile spreading from cheek to cheek.

"I think he's dead!" Charles said hopefully.

But he wasn't.

Eugene's chest rose into the air, his fingers clutched into a fist, his face morphing into a snarl, his entire body contorting and wriggling until he was standing, his breath heavy, heaving, panting, sweating.

His eyes grew wide and red.

His body grew muscle that wasn't there before.

His breath exuded from his lips in a grateful snarl.

"You pleased for my death, were you?" Eugene said, his posh voice mixed with the sinister low-pitched rumble of an earthquake.

"N – n – no!"

Eugene grabbed Charles by the throat and lifted him into the air.

"I think you were."

He squeezed his fist and Charles choked. Charles tried battering against Eugene's arm, but it was like a rat wriggling in a human's fist.

Charles's throat snapped and his head lilted to the side.

Eugene dropped Charles and turned to the other scientists.

In less than a minute he walked out of the laboratory, a bloody mess left behind him.

Chapter Twenty-Eight

A few heavy steps and the slamming of the basement door preceded Gus's entry to the kitchen.

"How's it going?" Desert asked. "You best friends yet?"

At first, Gus ignored the comment. Then he decided he wasn't prepared to take any grief from her, and he launched a glass that she quickly dodged and watched smash into the wall behind her.

"Jesus!" she said.

"Baby steps," Gus grunted, taking a few swigs of water.

"Look, Gus, I–"

"If the next words out of your mouth are another taunt or argument or any kind of bullshit then keep them."

"It wasn't, I was just going to say–"

"Oh my god," Whizzo declared, interrupting both of them. He quickly began sifting through the rest of the paper, finding lists of drugs.

"What?" Gus asked.

"This is it. This is what they created. They used the infection, but they are better – this is what it was meant for. Sadie was the beginning, she..."

Whizzo trailed off. Looked through a few more sheets of paper.

"And there's this countdown I keep coming back to, for a few days' time. I just don't get what it means."

"Let me ask you a question," Gus said. "Is there anything about his daughter in there? Records of her being lost in London?"

"Yeah, actually, I think there is."

Whizzo sorted through another few pages and found it.

"Details of a mission statement. Gus Harvey and Donny Jevon going to London to rescue his daughter. Laney." He looked to Gus. "I thought she wasn't his daughter?"

"She wasn't. He just wanted a record of his daughter supposedly being in London when it was bombed."

"Who bombed it?" Whizzo asked, then realised he'd read something about this, and sifted eagerly through a few more pages.

"Some of his allies."

"Here it is," Whizzo said. "China, France, among a few – but it doesn't say they were allies. It records their bombing of London as an attack."

"No, no – London was quarantined, and they wanted to get rid of all the infected that were in there. He arranged for the bombs to go off and I had two days to get his daughter before the allies destroyed it. Well, his fake daughter."

"So why would it say here that they attacked if he asked for them to do it?"

The question hung on the air like potent stench. Gus and Whizzo looked confused, but Desert had a different expression. One of horrified realisation. Like the truth was finally settling.

"What?" Gus asked.

"What is it?" Whizzo said.

"Eugene Squire..." Desert said, trying to find the words. "He wanted the record of his daughter being in London when they bombed it so it could look personal, so there was record of the bombing. But there's no record of the allegiance, just..."

She trailed off, her face twisting between expressions of confusion and understanding.

"What are you onto?" Whizzo prompted.

"I think I know what the army is for," Desert announced.

"What? What is it for?"

"Eugene wanted to create an image that London was attacked so that he could have an excuse to retaliate."

"To retaliate?"

"Yes. He's going to invade. He's going to cite this as his reason and invade, and with the army he's got, he's certain to win. They would have no defence." Desert looked to the other two and saw their absent agreement. "My God..."

No one spoke.

Minutes went by.

Then Whizzo suddenly recalled something else.

"Oh shit," he exclaimed.

"What?" Desert asked.

"The countdown I keep seeing, the one for two days' time..."

"You don't think...?"

Whizzo looked between Desert and Gus.

"Two days?" Gus repeated.

Whizzo nodded.

That was it.

Two days.

If the United Nations still existed, they would be unlikely to object, given the apparent attack on London.

Forty-eight hours was all that stood between Eugene Squire and everything he had planned for.

Forty-eight hours and that army would march into the rest of the world and kill off anyone the infected already hadn't.

Forty-eight hours, and there was nothing four helpless survivors could do about it.

48 HOURS

Chapter Twenty-Nine

Eugene stood over the army, in the same room and at the same window he often did. He didn't feel the need to sleep, there was too much adrenaline running through him, too much excitement.

At school, he'd been the dweeb.

At university, he'd been the nerd.

And even as a leader, he only demanded respect because of the muscle he owned, not had.

Everything had changed.

Everything.

The door opened and General Boris Hayes entered, rushing, a sense of urgency immediately apparent.

"Eugene," Hayes said. "There's been an attack."

"It's Mr Squire," Eugene decided.

"Excuse me?"

Eugene turned toward Hayes, enjoying the look of confusion.

"I said, it's Mr Squire."

"Fine, Mr Squire, Eugene, whatever – there's been an attack in the laboratory. All the scientists are dead."

"Are they now?"

"Yes, we need you to come look. Now."

Eugene chuckled, unable to help beaming, a smile of dramatic irony. Oh, how much he had respected Hayes. Relied upon him. Needed him.

Now Hayes was the one who needed him.

"Eugene?" Hayes prompted, confused, then corrected himself. "Mr Squire, I mean?"

Hayes approached Eugene, edging forward with an air of caution. Something about Eugene was making him worry and Eugene enjoyed it. He hadn't seen a man like Hayes be afraid of him before, and he wanted to relish every second of it.

"Are you coming?"

"It's such a nice night, Boris. Why not just enjoy it?"

"I don't think you understand."

"Oh, I understand. There's been an attack. In the laboratory. All the scientists are dead. That correct?"

Hayes considered this, then nodded, still confused.

"Er, yeah... correct."

"Marvellous. Is that everything?"

Hayes looked around himself, perplexed and wary.

"What's going on?" he asked.

Eugene grinned and turned back to the army, watching them work through the night.

"Come, stand with me, Boris."

Hayes did so, reluctantly. Stepping forward, precisely, foot by foot, until he was at Eugene's side, watching him.

"Do you know something about the attack?" Hayes asked.

"Whatever would make you think that?"

"I, just...you're not panicking. This would be something to be concerned about. What if it's Gus Harvey?"

"Gus Harvey isn't a threat anymore."

Hayes went to speak, then didn't. What could he say?

Eugene let out a laugh. He was enjoying this too much.

"See this army?" Eugene said. "They are all at my beck and call. I tell them to fight, they do it. I tell them to stop, they do it. I tell them to die, they do it. Until now, I thought that was the greatest power that existed to man."

"What?" Hayes said, looking from the army to Eugene, to the army, to Eugene. "What's going on?"

Eugene turned to Hayes and looked him up and down. He wasn't so intimidating after all.

"Thing is, though – don't you find yourself at a loose end?"

"Excuse me?"

"Well, this is my army. I command them. Your army is defunct as a result. You are the leader of nothing. What is the point of you?"

"Well, I would hope that I serve you in other ways."

"And, oh, you do. Well, you have. You have been my immediate muscle when the army haven't been at my side."

He took a step forward, and Hayes retreated a step backwards.

"But, see, I don't need that now. Not anymore."

"I don't understand, what are you–"

Eugene grabbed Hayes by the back of the head and slammed it into the table. Not knowing his own strength, he smashed the table, and shook with pride.

Hayes did not get up. At first, anyway. He attempted push himself up, but his hands were already sliding on his own blood.

Eugene lifted Hayes by the back of the neck and gaped at the mangled face he had created with one swift action.

Eugene shook his head.

Not so tough.

Eugene plunged Hayes through a nearby wooden chair.

He turned Hayes over and mounted him.

Hayes was too out of it and too groggy to know what was happening. His eyes were closed with occasional attempts to blink the blood out of his face. His nose was slanted to the side and most of his teeth were missing.

Eugene didn't waste any time.

He put his hands around Hayes's neck and squeezed. He didn't even need to strangle him hard – Hayes's neck snapped and his oesophagus squished until it was too collapsed for air to pass through.

Eugene stood and watched Hayes choke on breath that didn't come, spluttering until his body fell limp.

Wow.

What a rush.

That felt good.

Boy, did it feel good.

Chapter Thirty

No words needed to be spoken for Whizzo and Desert to know what the other was thinking.

They both stood outside the basement door, listening to Gus's voice. His voice was calm and expressive, reading a book with more passion than they had ever heard from him before.

"He's been at it for hours," Whizzo pointed out.

"This is ridiculous," Desert added. "We have days – in fact, not even that, we have hours – and this is what he's doing?"

Whizzo didn't respond. He agreed with the statement, he just refused to add to any more conflict.

"Maybe we should just go without him?" Desert suggested. "Take them on without him and Sadie?"

They glanced at Sadie through the door to what was once a living room. She was curled up on the sofa, despite the exposed springs and thick layer of dust.

"Are you kidding?" Whizzo said. "We wouldn't last a minute without them."

"And you think we'd last a minute with them? You think he isn't a hinderance?"

"So what's your plan, huh? We just march up there, the two of us, and start a fight with an army of superior beings?"

"And what would the plan be if Gus wasn't being delusional nutjob?"

Whizzo sighed. Bowed his head. Gus had reached a particularly riveting part of the story, and his voice became even more animated. The zombie's groans and murmurs grew louder, as if matching Gus's energy.

Whizzo sauntered away from the door. He didn't want to hear any more. Desert was right. Gus was desperate. And Whizzo was...

What?

What was he?

Caught somewhere between everyone else's war, trying to fight the war that was most important?

They were failing, and they stood little chance even if everyone was at their best. But with Desert's constant tirade and Gus's absurd obsession, it seemed as if fighting was futile.

Why was it up to them anyway?

"Where are you going?" Desert asked.

Whizzo paused by the living room door, watching Sadie.

Where was he going?

Gus's voice paused. Nothing but the groans came from the basement. They both listened, waiting to hear what was happening. After a minute or so, heavy footsteps stomped up the steps.

He appeared from the doorway and looked at Whizzo and Desert.

"Need water," he grunted. He walked purposefully to the kitchen and took a few swigs from the container.

He past them once again en route to the living room, where he found a CD player and a few CDs in the corner.

"Saw this earlier," he muttered. "Thought it might be worth a shot. Let's hope the batteries still have life in them."

He brushed the dirt off the speakers and lifted the CD player's lid, checking if there was a CD in it, and returned to the basement.

He paused in the doorway and looked back at the other two. They were gazing at him warily, yet expectantly.

"What?" he said.

They both hesitated.

"We need to figure out what to do," Whizzo said.

Gus looked between them both. "Okay," he said, shrugging.

"And we need your help."

"What the hell am I meant to do? You're the genius." He looked at Desert. "You're the stubborn killer. Why's it got to be up to me?"

"It isn't, we just...we think your time would be better spent–"

"Doing what?" Gus demanded, taking a step forward, his body arching.

When neither of them replied, he returned to the basement, slamming the door behind him. His footsteps stomped down the steps, followed by a moment of silence, and the reading began again.

Desert and Whizzo looked at each other. Whizzo went to speak but didn't. They just held each other's stare, knowing they were thinking the same thing.

"Come on," he said. "Let's try and figure this out."

"How?"

"I don't know. We just...need to try."

Whizzo returned to the table in the kitchen and went back through pages he'd already read numerous times. He felt Desert watching him but he didn't look up. He didn't want another conversation about Gus or about the stakes or about the risk or about what was going to happen.

He just wanted to do his bit to help.

He felt useless at the best of times. Combat wasn't his skill – *this* was his skill.

And with the lack of ideas, he was failing mightily at that.

36 HOURS

Chapter Thirty-One

Desert strolled leisurely into the living room – far more leisurely than she should be strolling.

But what could she do?

Whizzo was doing his part. Gus was going crazy.

And here was Sadie – laying on a broken armchair, completely peaceful, despite the number of broken springs digging into her back and damp spots marking the cushions.

Sadie awoke gently and lifted her head, looking at Desert. There was no panic or alertness, just the relaxed look of a person waking from a brief nap.

"Hey," Desert said.

Sadie smiled back. Which was fine, it wasn't like Sadie spoke much – and it wasn't like Desert particularly needed a conversation.

Maybe she could use this time effectively. Utilise what time they had to do something that may benefit them in the future. Teach Sadie something worth knowing.

What about CPR?

Sadie was a great fighter, but it would be good for her to know how to resuscitate one them if need be.

"You busy?" Desert asked.

Sadie looked back with those wide, innocent eyes.

"Want me to teach you CPR?"

Sadie looked perplexed.

"Erm... it's when you bring someone back to life after they stop breathing. Could be useful."

Sadie shrugged. Desert wasn't sure if this was a non-committal shrug of *whatever*, or a shrug because she didn't understand.

Desert knelt on the floor.

"Come here, and I'll show you."

Sadie leapt from the chair and crawled over to Desert, looking at her with the eagerness of a faithful pet.

"So, what you do..."

Desert looked around. She took a large, ripped cushion from the sofa and put it on the floor.

"Let's pretend this is our person who's dying. So this cushion is a person who's suffocating. Can't breathe. Yeah?"

A pause, then Sadie nodded.

"So first thing we do is check the heart, keep it beating. So we put our fists together like this."

Desert interlocked her two hands.

Sadie watched.

"Can you do that?"

Sadie still just watched. Desert nodded to Sadie's hands and Sadie slowly them into an identical position.

"Then we lift them above our heads like this," Desert said, lifting her hands above her head.

Sadie gave a vacant look then copied.

"And we bring them down, like this," Desert said, bringing her fists down upon the cushion.

Sadie looked slightly perplexed, and unlocked her hands.

"Right..." Desert pondered, then decided she'd go on regardless. "That's on the person's chest, yeah? Their chest."

She patted her own chest.

Sadie paused, then nodded. Desert had no idea whether this meant that she understood or not.

"Then we give them more oxygen. So say this part of the cushion is the face, okay?" Desert moved to the top of the cushion and looked at Sadie.

Sadie paused, then nodded.

"We pinch their nose, and breathe out long, hard breaths."

Desert pretended to pinch a nose, then moved her head down and pushed out a long, hard breath. She moved her head back, choking from the dust, which prompted Sadie to giggle.

"A few more of them, and this should be the point when someone would wake up. Do you want to have a go?"

Sadie paused, then nodded.

Desert waited, but Sadie did nothing.

"Are you having a go?"

Sadie continued to look back at her blankly.

It was useless.

Maybe it was only Gus that Sadie understood.

"Never mind," muttered Desert, and she left the room.

Chapter Thirty-Two

G us dropped the book.

The final word was read and it was done.

The images of his daughter left and the gangrenous, mutilated, pale monstrosity before him remained.

Still snapping.

Still pulling.

Still grasping and contorting and wriggling and writhing and desperately trying to reach Gus's flesh with its greasy, stinking hands.

No sign of humanity whatsoever.

Gus sighed.

Dropped his head to his hands.

This is so stupid.

He wouldn't admit it to the other two. In fact, he would stubbornly assert that this was a great idea, despite the time pressure and despite the stakes and despite the severity of the situation.

But he knew it.

I don't stand a chance.

How foolish he must look.

The others were probably up there laughing at him. Making fun. Chuckling heartily at his expense.

Oh, what an idiot, reading a book to a zombie.

Oh, what a numpty, smiling and playing nice to the infected.

Oh, what a hinderance, what a pointless man, what a disappointment to the cause.

He stood. Stretched his legs. He could do with a break but there was no time.

He took the CD player he'd found upstairs and placed it atop a few broken boxes. He pressed the on button and, to his surprise, it switched on.

Then again, why was it so surprising? Wasn't like there was anyone here to wear the batteries out...

He pressed play, no idea what music was about to start.

It was something classical. Beethoven or Tchaikovsky or something like that. Something cultured.

Something that he'd never listen to, but appreciated.

It reached a crescendo and he could feel the emotion of the orchestra. He closed his eyes and let it overcome him, let it pulsate through his body.

He looked to the zombie.

It paused.

Stopped snapping. Stopped groaning. Stopped reaching out.

Was this it?

Was it learning?

Gus smiled, stepping toward it eagerly, and–

Its yellow teeth clamped down as it thought it had hold of Gus's hand. A few teeth fell from its mouth upon the strength of the snap.

The music built to a harmonious melody and belted out of the weak speakers, and the infected just kept reaching out and trying and grabbing and failing like it had been doing for so long already.

Gus had to keep his resolve.

Had to smile. Talk. Be nice.

"What's the matter?" he said cutely – or, at least, as cute as his gruff voice was able. "Come on, I know you're enjoying it."

Snap. Grasp. Snarl.

"Are you listening to the music? Are you?"

Groan. Moan. Glare.

"Is it nice?"

A bigger snarl, a desperate grasp, a guttural moan.

"Oh, for fuck's sake," Gus said, turning away from the infected and marching to the other wall of the confined basement.

He leant his head against the damp brick.

How much longer was he going to give this?

How much longer did he have in him?

How much more could he hold back the progress of the group?

He started to give in. To understand why Desert resented him. To comprehend why they were so impatient.

This was getting ridiculous.

Pointless.

Absurd.

And they had less than a day and a half to go.

28 HOURS

Chapter Thirty-Three

Gus could feel their eyes on him, but he did not return their look. He merely sauntered into the kitchen and paused over the sink, dropping his head, closing his eyes.

He needed to get a grip on himself.

He needed to decide what the hell he was doing.

Reading to a zombie?

Playing music to a zombie?

And worst of all, getting annoyed with that zombie for not responding?

Jesus...

He huffed. Turned the tap but no water came out.

He knew that.

He knew no water would come out.

So why was he turning the tap?

"You okay?"

Gus thought that was Desert's voice, but he could be wrong.

"Fine," he grunted.

"You two best friends yet?"

His fists tightened around the edge of the sink, his body

shaking, until he lifted his fist and exploded it into the cupboard, smashing a hole in the wood.

As if it wasn't shitty enough, he had to put up with taunts.

He turned toward them to find their expectant stares turning cautious. Or were they worried? Or full of trepidation?

Who really gives a crap anymore?

"You got something to say," Gus grunted, "then say it."

Desert sighed and forced a patronising, reluctant smile to her lips.

"You don't want me to say what I have to say."

"No, I want you to say it. I just want you to put up with what happens to you afterwards, too."

Desert bowed her head. Shook it. Turned to Whizzo who sat over her shoulder, his hands in tufts of his hair and looking as exasperated as he ever had.

"You're a liability," Desert said. "You're losing it."

Gus shrugged.

"And so what if I am?"

"Don't you think we have a few pressing issues to deal with?"

Gus shook his head and began his march out of the room.

"I'm not putting up with this shit," he declared.

"Then now what?" Desert said, her voice weakening under her forced confidence. "Continue to bury your head in the sand as World War Three begins?"

Gus let out a sinister, sarcastic chuckle, pausing in the doorway.

"In case you haven't noticed," he said. "The world has already gone to shit."

"Then that's it, is it? The world's gone and there's nothing worth doing?"

"I *am* doing something."

"Singing songs with a zombie isn't something."

Gus charged forward, grabbed Desert by the throat and

kept charging until he reached the wall. He pinned her to it, ignoring her pathetic attempts to batter down his arm, watching her be completely helpless to his strength, relieving the aggression he'd been harnessing – this would shut her up. This would silence her. This would show her who you don't fuck with.

"I am getting sick of your whining," Gus said, his face an inch from Desert's, his warm, putrid breath blowing all over her face. "I am getting sick of your moaning. I am getting sick of your general shit. You want to go fight them without me, be my fucking guest. Either way, shut the hell up."

Gus threw her to her knees and stood back.

Desert grabbed her throat, stroking it, choking on air. Whizzo was immediately at her side, an arm around her. He helped her onto her back and leant her against the wall.

He looked up at Gus, who was still red-faced, fists clenched, panting – his wrathful eyes weakening as he began to see what he had done.

"You really are a prick," Whizzo said.

Gus closed his eyes and dropped his head.

Maybe if he kept them closed, he wouldn't have done that.

Stupid, stupid man.

The remaining few in the world who would still talk to him and this was what he did.

He turned to leave.

Sadie was in the doorway.

He stepped forward and she flinched back.

She looked scared, and that gave him a pain in his chest and a twist in his gut he was not expecting.

"Sadie…" he said, stepping forward again, to find her back away once more. "Sadie, I am not going to hurt you."

She shook her head and ran to Desert's side, where she crouched next to Whizzo, tucking her arms around Desert's waist.

"Maybe you should go back to your friend in the basement," Desert finally spoke, her voice hoarse as it gradually returned. "That's who you care most about. Isn't it?"

Gus didn't answer.

He simply took his cue to leave the room and return to the zombie below – the creature that would not care whether he read it a book or strangled it to death.

To the only monster in this house worse than him.

22 HOURS

Chapter Thirty-Four

Gus awoke, surprised at his sleep. Though he shouldn't have been – he was exhausted. He just never thought he'd fall asleep with one of the infected reaching for his face.

He rubbed his eyes. Leant forward. Ran his hands through his greasy hair.

He didn't want to look at it anymore.

He was tired of the greying facial features. He was sick of the chattering teeth, or at least those that remained. He was fed up, completely, of the scabbed fingers reaching out for him, constantly, so damn constantly.

And he was most tired of being wrong.

Of knowing he had a misguided belief that this could work.

Of hurting those around him with his stubbornness that Donny could be saved.

He lifted *The Ever-present*. Turned it over. Ran his hands over the dusty edges, feeling the rough corners and the tattered cover.

He could begin it again.

Read it from the first word.

To the final word.

And all through again.

But what would be the point?

He took in a big breath. Held it. Kept holding it.

Then let it go.

"What am I doing..." he muttered.

He stood.

Watched the zombie some more.

It had not changed its stance since the moment he brought it in and tied it to the drain pipe. It had not flinched in his persistent determination to get to him. It had not ceased in its hunger.

And he slowly began to admit the truth to himself.

This is not going to work.

The thought turned his morose, sombre mood to that of anger, wrath, and adrenaline.

He threw the book across the room.

"Why!" he screamed.

He grabbed the infected by the throat.

"Why won't you just–"

Just what?

What?

What was it this infected 'just' had to do?

He let its throat go, but only so he could retract his fist and lunge it through the stale jaw. It dislocated from the rest of its face, suffering from the gradual decay of its weakening body.

It was still not deterred.

He punched it again, exposing a cheek bone.

And again, bending its nose to the side.

Still, it persisted.

He kicked a nearby box.

Threw the chair across the room, gaining no satisfaction from its collapsing into various pieces of battered wood.

"Argh!" he growled, shouting, his throat growing rough and his voice breaking under his frustration.

Donny...

No!

No, no, no!

Donny had to be saved!

He ran back to the zombie and punched it in the gut.

"Why won't you feel?"

He swung his elbow against the back of its head.

"Why won't you react?"

He kicked its leg out. It fell to a crumpled mess on the floor, then pushed itself up and resumed its hungry reaching.

Gus fell to his knees. Tucked his head beneath his hands.

He refused to sob, but sobbed anyway.

Denial left the basement.

Realisation overcame the dark, dank smell of death and damp.

He finally admitted it.

Donny was going to have to die.

BEFORE

Chapter Thirty-Five

Tthe broken springs and wires of the mattress dug into the bones of Gus's back.

But it was all he deserved.

He flicked through the pages of *The Ever-present* like it meant something.

He even read a few of the pages aloud, as if his daughter was next to him. Curled into the curve of his arm, her head resting on his chest, falling asleep but refusing to not be awake.

But she wasn't.

And he no longer felt the pain. He felt numb.

And that made him hate himself even more.

He did not want to lose the pain. He did not want to ignore the agony, or reject the despair – as, if he did that, it would be like they were never alive.

The pain was what kept them fresh; what meant they still lived, and the memory stayed strong.

If he died, no one would ever know his family had once lived.

That was the one thing stopping him from taking the gun

he'd left haphazardly on the floor atop a pile of dirty t-shirts and doing what temptation called him to do every damn day.

He would end it at some point.

But he wanted to remember them first.

Of course, there was the possibility of heaven. If zombies could exist, so could God. He could slit his wrists and walk into the afterlife like it was a leisurely Sunday afternoon stroll to the park.

But, knowing his luck, heaven was what he always thought it was – utter shite.

He wouldn't die and go to an afterlife. No god would be there to take care of him. There'd be no reuniting with his family.

Everything would just stop.

End.

Nada.

Finito.

Done.

And that would be his legacy. The beautiful entry of death and his morbid exit from existence.

He closed his eyes and they were there. His wife's divine scent lingering over him as her hair brushed against his face. Straddling. Ready to take him to the place only she could.

But he opened his eyes and it was all a lie.

Laney was there. Begging for him to read the book, pulling on his hand, her hands so small against his.

But she wasn't there.

It was a lie.

There was nothing pulling on his hand. It was just the power of his imagination and the strength of his pain.

He opened the book.

What purpose did this book have now?

Why did he keep it?

Because he hoped to read it to Laney again one day?

So stupid.

It was as if, by letting that book fall out the window or fly onto a fire, he'd be removing all possibility of seeing her eager eyes light up as he read it once more.

This book no longer had a function.

He no longer had a function.

The world was ending and he didn't care.

He wished himself dead. Wished himself back to his family.

But he knew it was pointless.

All of it was pointless.

He dropped the book on the floor, hoping it would one day save someone else's life.

But it wouldn't.

It was just a book.

It was not his daughter.

21 HOURS

Chapter Thirty-Six

A shameful trudge up the stairs was to precede what Gus had always refused to give.

An apology.

Even his wife had come to terms with Gus's lack of requests for forgiveness. It wasn't that he never felt remorse, but that he could never utter the words *I'm sorry,* as if there was some kind of weakness in them, as if his stubbornness wouldn't allow him to feel the shame that those words would bring.

He understood the cautious looks directed his way as he entered the room; though Desert's look was beyond cautious, even beyond resentful – it was scalding, wrathful, eyes of searing hatred.

Fair enough, he supposed.

In her position he would do more than glare.

He went to apologise then didn't. It was more difficult than he was prepared to admit. In the end, he gave a huff, closed his eyes, and just came out with it.

"I'm sorry."

He waited for the words to settle like dust after a bomb,

then opened his eyes to find the looks his way had yet to change.

"You were right," he told Desert. "You were. I get that now. Donny, he... he can't be saved."

"Your friend not being friendly with you?" Desert snapped. "Your friend not–"

"Don't taunt me or I'll feed you to him."

Gus sighed as soon as he'd said it. He shouldn't expect any other reaction. He knew his apology was far from over, and this didn't help.

"It just... Donny was..."

"We've all lost friends, Gus," Whizzo interjected.

"Donny was more than just a friend. Donny was the one who showed me what it was to live. To care about something again."

Sadie emerged into the room.

"You both were," Gus told her.

He gave a weak smile, a hopeful smile that she would approach him. She did, though slowly, and he held out an arm for her. She tucked under the arm and rested her head in the curve beneath his shoulder, then reluctantly placed her arms around his waist.

"I'm sorry, Sadie," Gus whispered.

Now that was an apology that wasn't difficult.

Sadie was never someone he'd be content with upsetting, whether directly or indirectly.

She was as good a saviour to him as Donny was.

"So what do we do now?" Desert said, an air of scepticism inevitably remaining.

Gus shrugged and turned to Whizzo.

"Have we got anything we can use?" he asked. "Any ideas?"

Whizzo shook his head.

"How long have we got?"

"I'd estimate at less than a day."

Gus dropped his head. What a liability he'd been. He'd ruined their chances by remaining on his own useless mission, adamant that the impossible could be done.

"I don't know what to do," Gus admitted. "I don't. Is there anything we actually *can* do?"

"Bomb the place?" Desert suggested.

Gus flinched, instinctively rejecting the idea in case harm came to Donny. Then he told himself he was going to have to overcome that.

"There's no way we could find that kind of bomb power in such little time," Gus said.

"What are we going to do about the thing in the basement?" Whizzo said.

Gus nodded. Yeah, he guessed that thing was going to have to go.

"Why don't you do it?" Gus said. "It'll be good for you to take one down. It's tied up, you'll be fine."

Whizzo looked between Desert and Gus, fearful and wide-eyed.

Desert handed him her large hunter's knife.

"Okay," he said, his voice higher pitched than he intended. "Okay, I can do this."

He stood. Composed himself. Edged warily to the basement, pausing outside the door.

He opened the door and his footsteps were heard tapping down the stairs.

But no snarls. No groans.

Maybe the thing had starved to death already.

Gus stepped toward Desert. In an overwhelming surge of bravery, he held a hand out, offering it to her for the handshake.

She looked at it like he was offering her shit on toast.

"Come on," Gus urged her. "I've admitted I was wrong. Don't make this any harder."

"Any harder? Do you realise—"

"I do. Please."

She sighed. Held a limp hand out and gave a weak handshake.

"Thank you," Gus said. "Now, any idea on–"

"Guys!" Whizzo's voice called out.

Gus immediately grabbed a gun from the counter behind him, ready to run to Whizzo's aid.

"Guys, you might want to come and see this!"

But Whizzo's voice wasn't scared, wary or frightened.

It was confused and hopeful.

With an odd glance at one another, Gus, Desert and Sadie ran to the basement and down the stairs.

When they were at Whizzo's side, they marvelled at a sight that they never thought they'd see.

Chapter Thirty-Seven

Stunned, dumb disbelief greeted the sight of a dormant zombie, as placid as a curious child.

Its jaws no longer snapped, its hands no longer reached, and its mouth no longer groaned.

It just stood, idle, as if it didn't know what to do. Sniffing *The Ever-present*. Looking around at the room, searching for something but never finding it.

"What the..." Desert's voice muttered.

Whizzo murmured some sort of agreeance.

Gus stepped forward.

"Wait!" Whizzo said, reaching out for him – but Gus raised a hand and waved it away.

He poised, just out of reach of the infected, watching its movements; disjointed and chaotic, and never standing still – but never moving quickly.

With a large, confident intake of breath, he stepped within reach. The infected could, in any sudden movement, reach out and fasten its teeth around Gus's throat before he realised what was happening.

But it didn't.

The god damn thing didn't.

"I don't believe it..." he whispered.

"This – this isn't possible," Whizzo said.

Gus looked over his shoulder at Desert, who said nothing.

He didn't gloat. Just looked at her.

There was no satisfaction in winning – but satisfaction in proving to her that it could be done.

Sadie stepped forward. Sniffed the zombie. Looked back at Gus, as if to say, *I don't understand, this thing's harmless.*

"I'm going to take its restraints off," Gus said.

"No, don't!" Whizzo replied, backing away. "It might be tricking us!"

"The infected can't trick us."

"There are a lot of things we thought the infected couldn't do," Desert pointed out.

"Fine," Gus said. He took out his gun. "Happy?"

Desert withdrew hers too.

"Do it," she said.

Whizzo looked helplessly around himself, as if searching for a weapon, knowing he wouldn't be able to use one if he had it.

Sadie readied her hands – those gentle hands that could remove an infected's head as easy as poking the head off a sunflower

Warily, Gus reached for the cable tied around the drainpipe. He leant forward, his throat before its teeth, cut through it, and the thing was released.

They all stood back.

It stumbled forward, falling, then pushing itself up. Finding that it only had one leg, it pushed itself to its knee and dragged itself forward.

At first, Desert thought it was dragging itself toward her, and she aimed her gun – but with Gus's fervent shake of the hand, she realised it was aiming for the stairs behind her.

She moved out of the way and it pulled itself up one step,

then up another, until it was all the way to the top of the basement and dragging itself through the corridor.

They looked at each other and burst up the steps that sunk from the pressure of their running.

They followed it through the corridor. Its stale blood had dried and it left no puddle as it crawled to the front door.

"How is this even possible?" asked Desert.

"Reading. Music. All of it, it... it worked," Gus said, hardly able to believe he was saying it.

Gus opened the front door and let it out.

"Should we let it go?" Whizzo asked.

"Why?" Gus replied.

"I mean, we know it's not hurt us, but it's still the infected. We don't know how long this could last, or whether it's just us. It could harm someone else."

Gus watched thoughtfully as the infected dragged its heavy, one-legged body through a broken fence and across the overgrown grass of a nearby field.

"Look at it," he said, gesticulating with his hand toward its condition. "That ain't harming anyone."

And he shut the door, leaving the lone zombie to find its way into the world.

19 HOURS

Chapter Thirty-Eight

"We still need a plan," said Desert, getting straight to the point.

"You're right," Gus said, smiling at the surprised look on Whizzo's face, who looked like he'd been expecting another fight. "There's two things we need to figure out. One of them is more important, I get that, but we need to cover both."

"Fine," Desert said.

"One, what to do with Donny? Two, what to do with the army? I'm all ears."

"Well," Whizzo said, "you could just tie Donny up and sing him songs and read him books."

Gus was sure that wasn't meant as patronising as it sounded.

"We don't have time," Gus said. "Nor do we have the ability to capture and restrain someone like Donny. We need something we could do there, in the fight, something I could say or do that... I don't know. Gets through to him."

"What you said about Doctor Janine Stanton seemed to get to him," Whizzo pointed out. "What about her?"

"Nah, it stopped him temporarily, it didn't stop him altogether. We need something bigger."

"You suggested he killed Stanton," Desert pointed out. "What about his guilt?"

Gus slammed his fist against the side. Jabbed his finger into the air. Looked to the others with eyes so wide and determined it looked like his brain may burst from his skull.

"I have it!" he declared, then paused, biting his lip, his face chewing as he mulled his idea over.

"Well...?" Whizzo said.

"I'm going to let him *kill* me."

Silence.

Long, uncomfortable, confused silence.

Desert and Whizzo glanced at each other, confirming with their eyes that they both heard correctly.

Whizzo went to speak, but even though his mouth opened no words were uttered.

Desert then tried, but failed.

Gus looked between them, awaiting a response, with everyone unsure what response to give.

"There's one slight problem," Whizzo eventually spoke.

"What?"

"Er... If you do that, won't you be, kind of, I don't know... *dead?*"

Gus shook his head adamantly.

"No, no! See, Donny won't actually kill me."

"He won't?"

"No, he'll go to, and he'll get pretty close – but the guilt, it will, I don't know... stop him."

"How can you be sure?" Desert said, looking as sceptical as she ever had.

"Well, I can't, can I? But I'm pretty certain."

"He nearly killed me."

"Yes, but you're not me, are you?"

Desert paused, as if there would be more explanation than that – when there wasn't, she added, "I don't follow."

"Donny cares for me."

"Cared," Desert pointed out. "Past tense."

"No, he does. I know. We saved each other's lives. You don't do that and not feel some kind of bond."

"I really don't..." Desert stopped herself, considered it, then waved her hands in the air. "Fine, whatever."

"I know you don't think it will work."

"I don't." Desert shrugged. "What do you want me to say? I think it's the most stupid idea you have ever had. And you've had some doozies."

"Guys," Whizzo said. "It doesn't matter. It still leaves us nowhere with the army."

Another silence descended. He was right.

Gus sat, leaning his head on his hand, chewing his finger.

Desert licked her lips, huffed, deeply contemplating.

Whizzo looked between them.

"Right, what do we know about them?" Gus mused. "There has to be a weakness, we just have to find it. What do we know?"

"Well," Whizzo responded, "they almost killed us, look superior in every way, chased us, nearly got us until–"

"That's it!"

Gus leapt up.

"What? Them nearly getting us?"

"Exactly!"

Whizzo shook his head, confused.

"Why did they only *nearly* get us?" Gus prompted.

"Because we got away."

"How?"

"We made it to the lake, and they–"

Whizzo stopped. Sudden knowledge illuminated the room.

Desert stood. Whizzo stood. Gus bounced from foot to foot, giddy.

"They can't handle water," Whizzo said. "They can't swim!"

"Exactly!"

"So, what do we do?" Desert said. "Just take them to the lake again and push them in? We still need an idea."

Gus nodded.

They were so close.

They had the answer to one question, they just needed the answer to another.

He paced from one side of the room to the other.

They had it, he knew it, the solution was there, right in front of them, he just had to find it.

Then he did.

"I got it!" Gus said, looking excitedly to Whizzo.

"What?" Whizzo said. "Why are you looking at me?"

"You know how you think you're useless?" Gus said, walking toward him and placing a proud hand on Whizzo's shoulder. "You know how you think that we're the muscle? That we're the ones who carry you?"

"Uh huh..."

"My friend, you have just proven yourself wrong."

Whizzo shared a confused look with Desert.

"What?" he asked.

"That water bomb you were creating a few days ago – remember it?"

"Yeah, the one that could take water vapour and expand it and..."

Whizzo grinned.

"How long would it take you to create enough?"

"Jeeze, I don't know... Days?"

"What if you didn't have days? What if you worked on it solidly for, I don't know, a few hours? How long would it take?"

"I guess... Twelve, fourteen hours maybe."

Gus smiled warmly. "Then that would give us a few more hours to take the fight to them. Wouldn't it?"

"How would we even transport them?"

"We have hours, I can go find a trolley or something."

"But how can we be sure it would kill them?" Desert asked. "They only die from a shot to the head. How can there be any guarantee?"

"We're not really working on any guarantees here," Gus pointed out.

"But I still need more than a probably."

A few moments of thought went by.

"Just hypothesising," Whizzo said, "but there is no supernatural aspect to these zombies, they aren't magic – they are just infected. Yet it takes a shot to the head to kill them. So how does this infection protect them from shots to the body?"

Blank looks returned his eager stare.

"The infection must spread to their body, to their skin, thickening it somehow, making it harder to penetrate. This doesn't mean that they can't die from their insides being hurt, it means to get to them you'd have to go to the head, or go inside of them... For example, flooding their bodies with water."

"You are a bloody genius!" Gus exclaimed.

Whizzo beamed back at him.

"Okay," said Gus. "Let's do this. We're ready!"

Whizzo's smile faded, his initial excitement ended, and he grew jittery. Suddenly it all became so real.

"That's a lot of pressure, I don't know if I can–"

"You can."

Gus had never been so sure.

They had the plan. That was the simple part.

Now they had to execute it.

2 HOURS

Chapter Thirty-Nine

The same hollow steps paraded down the hallway – but somehow, they seemed hollower and heavier.

Donny winced, knowing what was coming.

Every time those steps approached, every time the same chaotic bounce began from afar and drew gravely near, he knew.

The door swung open and the same silhouette appeared in the doorway.

The same, but different.

Bigger, somehow. Stockier. More confident. Not the shuffling wreck, but the striding monster.

"Donny," said Eugene, the same voice but grander.

Donny backed up against the padded wall of his cell. Flinched in preparation, staring in readiness.

"Oh, Donny," said Eugene.

Donny?

That was him.

He knew that.

At least, it used to be.

Who was he now?

What am I now?

"You have served me so well," continued Eugene. "So, so well. And I will be forever grateful. Honestly, I will – you were quite the creation."

Eugene paced forward and crouched before Donny. Donny tried to move, but a chain around his ankle restricted his movement.

"I mean that," Eugene continued, as patronising as ever, his eyes with a sinister glint more powerful than Donny could understand. "But I do not need you any longer."

Eugene took a deep, satisfactory breath and flexed his muscles.

"Look at me," he said. "Just look at me. I know I'm the same face, the same words – but I am not the same man. And you can see that. Can't you?"

Donny didn't answer.

"Can't you?" Eugene grabbed Donny's hair and pulled his head back. This exposed Donny's throat and Eugene looked at it the way a hungry man would look at cake.

Donny was used to being tormented, but he feared Eugene more in this moment than ever before.

He frantically nodded.

"This means I don't need you to defend me any longer," Eugene persisted. "In fact, I don't need anyone to defend me at all. Not only do I have an army to fight my fights for me, but now..."

Eugene stood. He lifted Donny by the throat, choking him, his feet dangling helplessly.

"Now look at this! Look at it! Look at what I'm doing to you! It's ridiculous! How am I even doing this?"

He cackled, looking around as if someone was going to agree with him.

"I only wish these walls weren't padded so they didn't cushion your fall."

He threw Donny across the room. Donny winced as Eugene

grabbed hold of the chain attached to his ankle, yanked it out the floor and pulled Donny toward him. Donny slid aimlessly toward his captor, and looked upwards, cowering.

Eugene wrapped the chain twice around Donny's throat. He dragged Donny across the room, Donny clutching at the metal choking him.

"Stop grabbing at it!" Eugene commanded, and Donny obeyed.

Eugene placed a foot on Donny's chest and pulled on the chain.

Donny gasped and choked and suffocated but he did nothing to stop it – he was told not to, and he would always obey.

I must always obey.

Eugene's lecherous grin spread even wider as he pulled and yanked, gaining a sense of sinister satisfaction in watching Donny suffer.

Donny's eyelids began to droop.

His body began to fall.

And a faint voice from outside called his name.

He listened. What was that?

It was a voice he knew, but who was it?

"Eugene!"

It couldn't be.

"Eugene Squire, come out and face me you piece of shit!"

"By George," Eugene whispered to Donny. "It's Gus Harvey, come to die."

Eugene didn't need to reveal anything yet. He could sit back and enjoy two old friends in a David vs Goliath fight to the end.

He loosened the chain and let Donny's throat open back up, and Donny wheezed on oxygen.

A gunshot.

"That's six of your men now!"

Eugene unwrapped the chain from Donny's throat.

"Get up, Donny," he instructed. Despite the desperate pain, Donny obeyed.

"Eugene Squire, come out!"

Eugene squeezed Donny's chin.

Why?

Because he could.

"Now kill, boy," he instructed. "Kill."

Chapter Forty

❧❧❧

The guards hadn't been difficult to dispose of. There were two waiting outside the nearest entrance and Gus had shot both as he approached.

Two more men came to greet him as he entered the building. He shot one as Sadie ran up, rolling to dodge a bullet and tripping the other. Once the guard had been tripped, Sadie dove upon him and landed her fist upon his oesophagus. She withdrew her knife and planted it into the man's throat.

"When did you learn to use knives?" Gus inquired.

Sadie smiled and shrugged.

"You do surprise me," Gus said. "That's still three one to me, though."

Sadie smiled a sneaky smile and ran on ahead, where two more guards were approaching. She stuck her knife into the gut of one, and span beneath the trigger of the other before sticking the knife into their throat.

She looked to Gus and smirked.

"Fine, three all," he admitted.

They charged through the corridor, Gus's gun raised, Sadie's knife ready.

"Eugene Squire!" Gus called out. "Eugene Squire, get out here you coward!"

They turned another corner and Gus instinctively shot a man point blank in the head, and Sadie disposed of another.

"Four," she said, grinning at Gus.

"Fine, but it's still a draw," Gus said.

They continued up a set of stairs and, before Gus could shoot the oncoming guard, Sadie had sprinted forward and sliced open his chest.

"Not fair!" Gus claimed, playfully. "I had my gun ready!"

Sadie giggled and ran ahead.

"Eugene!" Gus continued shouting.

Sadie dispatched another, and Gus regretted making this a competition.

"Eugene Squire, come out and face me you piece of shit!"

He shot another guard in the head.

"That's six of your men now!"

Sadie looked back at him.

"Yeah, and you have eight, whatever," he whispered.

He marched further down the hall. It was eerily silent. The corridors were a clinical white; sterile, and depressingly so. He could smell cleaning products in every turn, and he imagined that was to get rid of the potent smell of death that arose from the army's chambers.

"Eugene Squire, come out!" he shouted, and turned another corner.

A few footsteps prompted him to turn suddenly, alert and ready.

A shadow announced itself on the far wall, along with the face of a familiar friend.

Gus dropped his gun to his side.

"Donny," he acknowledged.

Donny looked back at him with eyes both weak and strong,

his body both ready and scared. There was a red mark across his neck, and old bruising over his face.

"What have they done to you?"

Donny didn't reply. He hovered where he was, swaying from foot to foot, waiting intently for something.

Gus threw his gun down the corridor behind him, away from them both. He held his hands in the air and looked expectantly at Donny.

"I'm unarmed," he pointed out. "You want the clean kill? You have it."

Donny stepped forward but did not yet attack.

Why?

What was he waiting for?

Gus looked to Sadie beside him.

"Go find Eugene Squire," he instructed her. "Kill him. Do it now."

Sadie nodded and continued to run down the corridor, leaving Gus alone with Donny.

"It's just us now," Gus said, and began stepping ever so slowly toward Donny, his hands raised. "Just us, Donny. You and me."

Donny's head slanted to the side. His nose curled up, his eyes squinting.

"That's it," Gus continued. "You remember me, don't you? Your friend."

Gus was so close now he could reach out and touch Donny. But he didn't. He kept edging, kept his hands in the air.

"You saved my life," Gus said. "Not just in coming back for me with those cannibals, but in giving me purpose. You remember?"

He stood within Donny's personal space, so close. He could not decipher the look on Donny's face, what it was, what he was thinking – but there was something going on behind those weary eyes.

"You're my friend, Donny."

Gus began to lower a hand, slowly, toward Donny's shoulder.

"And I've come back to take you home," Gus said.

As soon as the lightest touch settled upon Donny's shoulder, Donny grabbed Gus's wrist and twisted it to the side, taking Gus to his knees.

He kept his eyes locked on Donny's.

Donny sent his fist into Gus's face, sending Gus to the floor.

Gus did not fight back.

Chapter Forty-One

Sadie ran.
Run.
Find Eugene.
Kill Eugene.

She did as she was asked, powering through the corridors, sniffing him out.

Eugene had done terrible things to her.

Terrible, terrible things.

Eugene bad.

Eugene evil.

Eugene...

She heard it, from the corridors she had run from.

Slamming.

Punching.

Hurting.

She paused.

Gus said find Eugene.

But Gus was getting hurt.

She could recognise his grunts better than anything, she knew what it was; she could even smell the blood.

She turned back, charging through the corridors, pounding off the walls, and she found them.

Donny above Gus's body, fist retracting then plunging, again and again, and again, and again. Finding its way through Gus's crooked nose. She could smell Gus's blood on Donny's knuckles, and she could see the state of Gus's face.

His eyes were closing.

What did this mean?

Gus hurt.

She leapt forward and took hold of Donny's head and pulled him away from Gus. Gus didn't come around. Didn't move. Just lay on the floor, so still, so unaware.

Donny pulled her off him and raised her into the air by her throat, until he was out of reach of her swiping hands, and he threw her into the far wall.

She lifted her head and saw him.

Further down the corridor, behind Donny.

Eugene Squire.

That's who she had to get.

That's who Gus had told her to...

She jumped to her feet and ran, but before she could pounce, Donny had a hold of her hair. He pulled her back, taking her off her feet and throwing her into the wall.

Sadie whimpered. She hadn't felt pain like this before.

Donny punched her, which knocked her off her feet.

He went to punch again, but didn't.

She turned her head. Gus was out of focus, but he was standing.

A puddle formed beside his foot. Drops of red dripped from his nose. His face was mangled, his features slanting in all the wrong directions, the real-life version of a Picasso painting if that painting had been doused in blood.

"Knock it off," he said. The words melted on Sadie's ears but she understood them well enough.

Eugene's chuckle accompanied Gus's resurgence. It was ignored.

"It's me you were pummelling," Gus said, his voice deadening, croaky, as if hidden away in a box somewhere.

Donny stepped toward Gus.

"Well I ain't done being pummelled," Gus announced.

Donny kicked Gus's artificial leg to knock him back to the floor and dropped a knee into his chest. Gus coughed and rolled, but this did not deter Donny, who lay his fist once more into Gus's wretched face.

All through this, the pain was intensified by the agonising sound of Eugene's cocky chuckle.

Chapter Forty-Two

It was the same corridor they had crept along before – only it no longer had the sense of cautious curiosity it once had; instead, it felt more like an omen of death.

Whizzo and Desert both had a hold of a trolley that Gus had managed to acquire whilst Whizzo had been busy creating the water vapour bombs. The hours had gone by so quickly, Whizzo wasn't sure how Gus had managed to venture out, loot a DIY store, and return with such a utensil in the same time.

They paused as they reached the entrance, peering out at the training army. Eating, combat drills, and obedience training – all in their allocated parts of the vast room. The superior infected worked with such power and perseverance, their bodies still moving with inhuman jolts, and their human faces revealing monstrous eyes.

"Do they ever rest?" Desert whispered.

"I wondered that," Whizzo said. "I mean, have you ever seen a zombie sleep?"

Desert mused on this for a moment. She'd never thought about it, but it was a fair point. The zombie in the basement hadn't seemed to have had any rest over the last few days.

"Sadie does," Desert pointed out.

"Yeah, but is that out of necessity or boredom?" Whizzo questioned.

Desert went to continue this debate then decided it was better left for another time.

They each took a side of the first bomb. Whizzo had created them bigger than his prototype in an attempt to create a larger wave upon explosion. Honestly, he had no idea whether these things were actually going to work like he thought they would; it wasn't like they'd had time to test them.

But he hadn't pointed this out.

What would be the point?

There was no other option, and to create doubt in the others when they'd placed such great faith in him was unfair.

Though who it was unfair to was unclear.

They crept along the edge of the room, the bomb between them, praying the army did not notice, and placed it in the room's corner.

Whizzo fixed a device to one of the bombs and clicked something.

"What's that?" Desert asked.

"Detonator," Whizzo responded, as if it was the most stupid question anyone could have asked. They crept silently out of the room and back into the corridor.

"Where now?"

Whizzo withdrew a few screwed up pieces of paper from his back pocket and spread them out on the floor. They were, or at least he believed them to be, blueprints of the compound. The layout looked similar enough, at least.

"Back out," Whizzo said, tracing his finger along the map and looking for the route to the next corner of the room via the outside of the compound. He had planned this, but that was before he'd spent many hours creating explosive water vapour devices – his memory wasn't quite catching up with him as quick as it was before.

Nevertheless, he led them both out and hoped for the best.

They trekked through the woods, moving far away from the building so as not to be noticed by snipers, and walked almost a mile until the next point. It would have easily been a few hundred yards along the building's perimeter, but they couldn't risk being seen, and a mile hadn't sounded so long when they weren't lugging around a giant trolley.

A sniper was atop the roof, settled in their position, looking over their path back inside.

They were going to walk right under their eyeline.

"What do we do?" Whizzo asked.

Desert peered at the sniper, thinking deeply. Whizzo watched her, no idea what to suggest, or if there was even anything to suggest.

"No idea," she admitted.

"That doesn't inspire hope."

She sighed. She did have an idea, but she was contemplating the many other non-existent ideas before she returned to the only idea she had.

"I'm going to have to provide a distraction," she said.

Whizzo was confused for a moment, then once he realised what she was planning to do, vigorously shook his head.

"What? No!"

"I need to draw his fire so you can get in."

"Don't be stupid."

"You just concentrate on getting the bomb in. Don't worry about me."

"I'm not letting you do this."

"Whizzo, you don't have a choice, I have to–"

"I do have a choice," he said decisively. "You get the damn bomb in, then there's a tunnel you can go through unnoticed. Meet me on the other side."

Without another word of discussion, he sprinted away from her.

She went to call his name, but didn't, knowing that would draw attention to both of them.

"Shit," she said instead, quietly and to herself.

She watched as Whizzo ran into the distance and became submerged amongst the trees.

"You idiot..."

She looked to the sniper.

As if Whizzo even knew how to distract them.

As if he even...

The sniper stood. He'd seen something.

He was looking the other way, however temporarily.

She had to trust him.

This was the moment.

Chapter Forty-Three

Such satisfaction came so rarely.

Taking the superior genetics and pumping it into himself – yes, that was good.

Killing Hayes as Hayes cried like a helpless morsel – yes, that was great. Hell, it was fucking brilliant.

But this...

This was *the tops*.

Standing aside, watching Gus Harvey get beaten to death by his old friend, now his adversary.

The only satisfaction missing was that Eugene wasn't doing the pummelling himself.

He was tempted to tap in. To move Donny out of the way and step in himself.

But what could be more satisfying than watching Gus die this way?

The proverbial thorn to his proverbial side.

The annoyance; the insistent, constant, badgering irritation – the fly that hovers around your face and won't be swatted away.

The hinderance to his scheme.

He should have had him killed when they were back in the facility. Back when he kept him alive for information that his scientists were perfectly able to deduce themselves.

Then again, he wouldn't have had the opportunity to watch this.

And watch it he did!

His deplorable, infamous grin widened. His arms shook with giddiness. His legs practically bounced with excitement.

Like a child meeting a puppy, he just didn't know what to do, there was too much to smile about!

Donny continued to pull back his fist and lay it into Gus's contorted face, squishing Gus's features and bending them in ways they should not be squished and bent.

Eugene did wish Donny had been more inventive.

It was like before the infection had spread, back when he used to watch films involving torture, and the captor just keep punching or working on the chest, and he'd sit there thinking...*amateurs*.

No, the real way to torture a man is to cut his dick off – as soon as the scissors were placed beside the shaft he'd tell you his wife's bra size for all you cared.

But no, Donny was still just focussing on the face. The face was becoming a bloody, unrecognisable mess, yes, but it was still not as creative as Eugene would be.

He looked at his watch.

He hadn't much longer.

As much as he was relishing this, they had things to do and places to be.

He sighed.

He didn't want to tell Donny to end it, he wanted it to carry on, he was enjoying it too much. Like when an awesome film comes to an end and you watch the credits thinking *why did that have to stop?*

But the credits needed to roll.

The curtain needed to fall.

And Eugene needed to invade a few countries with an army of superior geneticised beings.

He laughed.

What a thought...

"Donny," Eugene said.

Donny didn't look back. Too engrossed in his work. Such a good boy.

"Donny!" Eugene tried again.

Donny paused and looked back at him.

"That's enough," Eugene said. "Finish him so we can get on with our lives."

Donny nodded and turned back to Gus.

1 HOUR

Chapter Forty-Four

It was probably the stupidest decision Whizzo had ever made – and he'd made some stinkers.

He ran close enough that the sniper would spot him and, as soon as he saw the sniper rise from his seat, he retreated once more to the shelter of the trees.

The sniper took aim.

"Shit," he said.

I hope Desert knows what to do...

He ran in zigzags, creating a difficult target.

But surely the sniper would know what this was?

No one would normally run in zigzags beneath trees. Wouldn't the sniper realise that this was a diversion?

Fuck it.

He made the decision not to overthink every aspect of what he was doing and to just continue.

And, just as he found himself calming and growing confident in what he was doing, a quick whistle of wind then a tiny explosion of mud yards behind his feet stiffened his legs and shook his chest.

He fell. The trees and bushes and leaves all melded into a

green blur. The sky overhead burst a migraine-inducing light between the branches.

He'd never been shot at before.

And he needed to get up before he was shot at again.

"Come on, dickhead," he told himself. "Gus does this all the time."

He pushed himself to his feet and sprinted forward. He avoided zigzagging to cease any pattern to his running and ran erratically instead. He wondered if the sniper was watching, as he ran a good while without another shot.

Then one grazed his leg and sent him sprawling into the nearby bush.

It hurt like someone had smacked a hot, wet towel against his calf.

He pulled up his trouser leg. It was just a graze. A scrape of red. He had been lucky.

He pushed himself up again and ran. He refused to believe that the pain was there as, after all, it hadn't hit him properly – and Gus had run many times with a bullet lodged in his calf.

He glanced over his shoulder. He was halfway across the length of the compound, but the sniper was still there, nearly out of view but still aiming.

What if he went out of sight?

Would the sniper not alert others that he was there? Could he expect a parade of armed guards? Or even worse – could he expect the army?

He just had to hope that a single idiot like him was of such little concern that they wouldn't bother to pursue him. Considering that they were planning on invading multiple countries might be to his advantage – he wouldn't be important enough to worry about.

The sniper took one last shot, and it hit the tree just past his head.

He kept running and he was out of sight.

He still kept running.

What about Desert? Would she have found the tunnel?

He just had to rely on her, like she had relied on him. Be confident in the knowledge that she would make it. That she would be there, waiting for him, the bomb planted.

She could handle herself.

But not against an army of...

He shook his head and just kept running. It took him a few minutes of jumping over logs, ducking branches and stumbling over bushes, but he made it to the other side.

Two guards stood outside the entrance.

He stayed out of sight.

What about those two guards? Would she know they were there?

He had no way of telling her.

Why is she not here yet?

He suddenly had a desperate, grave, sinking feeling in his gut that this was a ridiculous mission. They didn't know if the devices he created were even going to work, never mind whether they would successfully accomplish the task of placing them at all four corners unnoticed.

Someone approached the door from the inside...

But they didn't.

It was just a flicker of light fooling his eager mind.

Could I help her?

He could take out those guards.

He shook his head.

Who am I kidding?

He couldn't take out anyone.

Then there was more movement. Another flicker of light? No, there was something.

The guards were distracted.

A bloody hole appeared in one of their foreheads, then the other, and they both fell.

Desert appeared from the door, pulling the trolley.

She looked around, just as terrified as he was, searching for him.

He appeared from the bushes and, immediately upon seeing each other, they ran into each other's arms and tightly embraced.

"Did you do it?" Whizzo asked.

"I did it," Desert answered. "One more to go."

They hugged for a little longer, then proceeded to the final corner of the building.

Chapter Forty-Five

"That's enough," said Eugene. "Finish him so we can get on with our lives."

A brief respite followed Eugene's instructions. Gus was able to roll onto his side and lay his cheek on the ground, to which it stuck. He pulled it off and saw a blur of blood beneath him, still dripping.

His mind was so groggy, a mess, like a hundred cluttered rooms full of junk. He couldn't find sense or understanding or thought; all he could find were vague wonders and distant pain.

Despite all of this, he managed to push himself to his knees. His left hand slipped in the puddle of his blood and he collapsed again, and he was sure he could hear laughing, but he pushed himself to his knees once more.

His arms wobbled. He couldn't keep himself steady.

He threw himself onto his back and leant against the wall. He allowed his eyes to close for a moment, allowing his awareness to return long enough for him to stop himself from passing out.

If he passed out, it was over.

He looked up.

There he was. The empty face of Donny. Out of focus and out of his mind.

"Kill him," said a voice.

It was Eugene Squire's.

Gus looked to his side. There was Sadie, laying on the floor, bloody, cowering, shaking, concussed.

"Kill him now," insisted Eugene.

"I love you, Donny," Gus said. It was the best he could think of and it only prompted further guffaws from Eugene.

Donny bent over Gus and withdrew the hunter's knife from his belt.

His own friend killing him with his own knife.

It was kind of poetic, in a way.

Donny pulled his arm back.

"Wait," Gus said, padding his jacket, feeling for something in his pockets.

"Hurry up, Donny," Eugene's voice said, angrier and more direct.

"Wait, I have something here..."

Donny swung his arm down, aiming the knife at Gus's throat.

Then he paused, the knife an inch away, looking at what Gus had taken from his pocket.

"What the hell are you doing?" Eugene shouted, unaltering abhorrence in his voice and his gestures. "I said kill him!"

Donny didn't retract the knife, nor did he push it further.

And Gus didn't move from its reach. If Donny so wished, that knife would be in and out of his throat with as little as a twitch.

But Donny was transfixed. Staring intently, beholding what was before him.

"I think..." Gus said, his voice weak, "that these... are yours..."

Gus held out the item to Donny.

A pair of sunglasses.

Donny stared at them. Gus's vision slowly returned, enough for him to see the conflict in Donny's face. His instructions and his programming rivalled by a sombre recollection.

"Remember them?" Gus said.

Donny didn't answer. Didn't move.

He looked horrified.

There was something working behind those eyes, something thinking, desperately wondering – *those sunglasses*.

What were they?

"That's it," Gus said. "You do remember."

He smiled, then stopped, his cheeks hurting from the movement.

Donny's expression turned to confusion, like he knew those sunglasses, but couldn't figure out where from.

"I got you them," Gus announced. "You were yapping on about sunglasses and how you wanted a cool pair of shades. I snapped at you. I was too pig-headed to apologise, so when I got petrol – there they were. And I picked them up for you and I'd never seen you looking so chuffed."

Donny's eyes rose to Gus's face. Still confused. Still perplexed.

"That's it," Gus said. "You remember me, don't you? Hard to recognise covered in blood, but you see me."

Donny's knife-wielding hand shook.

"Stab me if you wish," Gus said. "That's fine. Just make up your mind. Are you a killer, or are you Donny?"

His arm shook with more vigour. Wanting to push the knife forward and wanting to take it back.

"What the hell is this?" Eugene demanded. "I said kill him, so you damn well kill him!"

Donny's head turned to look at Eugene.

"You fucking imbecile, do as I say!"

Donny took the knife away.

He stood.

Straightened his back.

And he changed everything with one, single syllable:

"No."

Chapter Forty-Six

A single memory changed everything.

Donny could see it, like a cinema screen just out of reach, projecting onto the hazy canvas of his memories.

Those sunglasses...

Shades...

He'd been after a cool set of shades...

He wasn't cool, never had been. He was nerdy, geeky and annoying. But those sunglasses.

Gus had fetched them for him.

Gus.

Who is Gus?

Gus Harvey.

The one below him.

His face. Bloody. So bloody.

Who did that?

Did I do that?

"What the hell is this?"

A familiar voice.

A commanding voice.

"I said kill him, so you damn well kill him!"

He was right. Donny had to kill him.

Had to kill Gus Harvey.

Gus Harvey.

Why?

Who?

I don't understand...

He held the knife by the throat of the man who was...

Gus Harvey?

Yes, Gus Harvey.

Is that him?

Friend.

Friend?

Didn't matter.

Friend – but didn't matter.

Those shades.

My sunglasses...

He wanted to wear them.

Put them on. Look cool again.

No, not my job.

Kill.

Kill Gus Harvey.

He pushed the knife further and resisted. His arm wobbled, shaking his whole body, the knife banging back and forth.

Gus Harvey didn't move.

Just waited for the knife to meet his neck. To welcome death like an old friend.

An old friend.

Like an old friend...

"You fucking imbecile, do as I say!"

Do as he says?

Why?

Donny took the knife back. The quivering ended.

He stood.

Looked over his friend's bloody face.

He did that.

I did that.

Why did he do that?

He looked to Eugene Squire. The one behind him. The one who had beat him and hurt him and...

No more.

Never any more.

"No," Donny said, definitely and decisively.

"What!" Eugene shouted, shock and horror adorning his face; his uppity face; his smacked-arse face; that horrible, conniving face.

"I said no," Donny repeated.

What was he saying?

How was he saying that?

"Are you disobeying me?"

Donny looked back to Gus.

Dropped the knife.

Took the sunglasses.

Looked to the girl on the floor. Cowering. Also bloody.

"Friend..." she whispered. "Friend..."

He put the sunglasses on.

He felt so cool.

So fucking cool.

"So you're not going to kill him?" Eugene asked.

Donny shook his head.

"I am not," he answered.

"Fine," responded Eugene, stepping forward and picking up the knife Donny had dropped. "That's just fine."

Without a moment's thought or hesitation or a second for anyone to perceive what was happening before it happened, Eugene stuck the knife into Donny's gut and twisted it.

Chapter Forty-Seven

Eugene could hear the attempt to scream from Gus, but Gus's voice gave nothing more than a breath – something he wouldn't be able to give fairly shortly.

But first, the little rat boy.

The disobedient little shit.

The impudent piece of filth.

How dare he?

To say no to *him*!

To deny his conditioning, to override his training, to completely undermine the entire operation that twisted his mind because of a pair of measly little fucking sunglasses?

Eugene twisted the knife again, watching Donny's face as it knotted and grimaced and distorted and misshaped. His mouth hung open like a hungry dog, his eyes wide, a terrified piece of soon-to-be roadkill staring at a superior predator.

"No!" Gus shouted, his voice finally returning. He pushed himself to his feet and stumbled backwards but pushed himself up again.

Eugene wondered how Gus would even consider the possibility of standing a chance against him if Gus didn't even stand a chance against Donny – then he remembered that Gus didn't know. A few days ago, Eugene was a feeble dweeb Gus could easily squish.

Not now.

Oh, boy, not now.

Gus threw a punch at Eugene. Eugene didn't even falter. He caught the fist, then clamped his spare hand around Gus's neck, lifting him into the air.

"You idiot," Eugene spat. "You moron."

Eugene threw Gus at the wall.

Gus looked back, wide-eyed – a new wave of fear.

Gus hadn't expected this.

Eugene enjoyed his shock, delighted at it.

He took the knife from Donny's gut, then stuck it in again a few inches over.

Donny went to throw a feeble arm.

"Put your arms down, Donny," Eugene instructed, and Donny did as he was told.

"What have you done?" Gus gasped.

"What have I done?" Eugene repeated with as much gloating as he could force to his most unpleasant of voices – he may have become stronger, but his irritating voice still remained the same.

Gus stood and charged. Eugene punched him, sending him stumbling backwards once again.

Then something took Eugene by surprise. Which was stupid, really, as he knew she was there – but the girl who had been lying and cowering had leapt to her feet and jumped onto his back, causing him to step away from Donny, and allowing Donny to stumble backwards and rip the knife from his belly.

Donny fell, delirium causing him to collapse.

If Donny was the ratboy, then Sadie was undoubtedly the ratgirl. Bony, revolting features. Quite a pretty face, but dirty and grubby – the kind of animal his servants would have disposed of on his behalf.

As it was, he would enjoy disposing of her himself.

He grabbed her wrists and twisted them. She held on, but yelped from the pain. He grabbed her wrists tighter and she continued to yelp.

"Donny, Donny," he could hear Gus whimpering. "Donny, come on."

Eugene did not intend to deal with one problem before he'd dealt with the other.

He grabbed Sadie by the hair, pulled her off him, and threw her down the corridor. She stepped back to her feet and sprinted toward him.

He still had enough time.

Enough time, that was, to charge at Donny's suffering body.

Enough time to kick Gus out of the way.

And enough time to take his knife from Donny's limp hands and finish it with a slice across his throat.

The last few gasps of breath slipped past Donny's lips and his body fell into an empty slumber.

Eugene looked at his watch. He was running out of time.

But he could not deny himself the pleasure of showing off his grand abilities against these other two urchins.

He rolled up his sleeves.

This would not take long.

Chapter Forty-Eight

❧

They were in the fourth and final corner of the room – four more than Whizzo ever thought they'd manage. This corner, however, felt the most exposed.

There was nothing they could hide behind. Nothing to shield them or cover them. They were just hoping none of the army turned around.

They were paces away.

Training. Eating.

They were even more revolting up close. From afar they looked like humans with characteristics of the infected – this close, they looked not human at all.

They snarled upon every thrust, grunted upon every lunge, and slobbered upon every bite. They had the shape of a person, the body, the features – but none of them were remotely human. Their movements were jolted, like every action was the onset of a seizure – yet their movements were also executed with perfect precision. If they were a sonnet, it would be a mess of chaotic words that, when read aloud, sounded like the most articulate piece of poetry ever written.

"Jesus Christ," Whizzo said under his breath as they finished setting down the final bomb. "Just look at them."

"We best not," Desert advised. "We don't want them to look at us. Come on."

She crept back along the wall, searching for the passageway they had snuck along. They reached it just in time, and they both let out a relieved breath that they had made it unnoticed.

"Wait!" Whizzo yelped. "I didn't put the detonator on it!"

Desert looked at him and they both contemplated the same thing – *could we get away with this bomb not going off?*

They knew it greatly reduced the risk of success.

They knew this was more important than their lives.

But they also knew that they were just about to escape. One final sprint and they would be out, ready to hit the button and flood the entire compound from the ground up.

"I have to," Whizzo said, resolved and regretful. "We need them all to go off."

Desert sighed. Looked over his shoulder at the movement of bodies. Considered every possible way that they could avoid returning.

"We have no choice," Whizzo said, closing his eyes and hating himself as he said it.

He really did not want to go back.

He would do anything to not go back.

But he had to, and he knew that.

"You can wait here," Whizzo said.

"Are you kidding? I'm not letting you–"

"We're less likely to be noticed if there's just one of us. I'm short, I can sneak, I'll be fine."

Desert did not look convinced.

"Honestly," Whizzo insisted. "It'll be quicker."

Desert sighed and looked over Whizzo's shoulders once more.

"I'll be right back," Whizzo said, and instantly thought of

all those horror movies he used to watch where a character would say *I'll be right back*, only to never return.

He crouched, moving subtly and stealthily out of the door and staying against the wall. He remained unnoticed, but there was still a lot to do.

He realised he was holding his breath. Yet, even though he realised this, he did not let it go.

His footsteps were placed with the lightest tap, his hands guiding him against the wall with the largest quiver, and his eyes staring at the bomb he approached with the widest stare.

Once he arrived, he patted his body in an attempt to remember where he'd put the last detonator.

I didn't leave it with Desert... Tell me I didn't leave it with Desert...

He was not prepared to do this again.

Luckily, he found it in the depths of his back pocket. He reached out and placed it upon the side of the bomb.

He went to leave, but it didn't look right.

It was upside down.

Bemoaning his own stupidity once more, he went to remove the detonator in order to put it the right way up.

But it was stuck. It had fixed itself in place.

He pulled harder, but it did not come off.

He yanked and yanked, but it barely shook.

Finally, using all the strength he had, he pulled on the detonator and it fell to the floor, creating a large clatter.

His breath stuttered.

He looked into the room.

Heads turned his way. A few, then some more, then even more – until a hundred eyes were fixed on him.

A hundred dead, reddened, evil eyes.

Shit.

He slapped the detonator onto the bomb the correct way around and went to run.

He halted his run as he watched a few of the army stand to block him – and when he stopped, they stopped.

He looked to Desert, waiting in the passageway.

"Fuck it," he said, as he took out a device with a large button.

He pressed it and each corner of the room exploded with water.

Then he ran.

And they chased.

But it took seconds before he was caught up in the waves.

Chapter Forty-Nine

Despite the ever-aching, agonising pains shooting throughout every muscle of his body, the adrenaline gave Gus the burst he needed to dive to Donny's side and shake him and shake him and shake him and shake him until...

Everything he'd been fighting for.

Everything he'd been working on.

Wasted.

The life he'd saved, the life he'd picked from morbid obedience, from slavery – done.

Donny was...

Don't say it. Don't think it. Don't even...

Dead.

He's dead.

No matter how much Gus shook, Donny's eyes didn't move and his chest didn't rise. His body was somehow heavier, his face somehow angelic yet empty.

Gus looked up at Eugene.

Eugene Squire and his cocky chuckle, his dirty leer, his ugly face that provoked such wrath, such anger.

"You..." Gus growled.

I am going to kill you.

Sadie sat in a ball, huddled up, her arms around her shaking knees, staring at Donny.

Gus pushed himself to his feet.

How did Eugene even manage to do that?

Eugene was a weakling.

He was...

"My God," Gus gasped, looking Eugene up and down with the little clarity his squinting black eyes would allow. "What did you do..."

Gus was surprised that he was surprised.

Eugene Squire was a coward. He needed to infect himself to give him any chance.

Unfortunately, Gus knew how little chance this left him.

"That's it," Eugene said. "That's it, Gus Harvey. I can see it dawning on you. I can see it settling over you like a black cloud. I can see your thick, mediocre brain chugging along, figuring it out. However did I do this? And yes, there it is. You know. Don't you?"

"You're a sick bastard."

"Am I?" Eugene stuck out his bottom lip as if to consider this suggestion. "What would you do, if you were granted the power to be stronger than anyone else in the world?"

"I'd say no thanks, I don't need it. And then I'd carry on with my life."

Eugene took a step toward him.

"Liar."

Gus looked to Sadie, who was cowering.

To Donny's body.

To the twisted monster above him.

"You want revenge," Eugene said. "I can see it. But you're thinking... however can you compete with me now?"

"That is not what I'm thinking."

"No?"

Gus took a step toward Eugene.

"I'm thinking, man, this prissy little posh prick is going to die."

Gus swung his fist, using as much leverage as he was able to attain, packing all his strength into it, lunging his beefy knuckles, and smacked it through Eugene's cheek.

Eugene's head turned with the impact, but only slightly. He brushed himself off.

Gus went to swing again, but Eugene had swung before he'd even managed, and he was against the wall and on his arse before he even realised what had happened.

"Fuck, man," Gus muttered. He was losing energy. The fight inside of him remained, but his body could not attest to that. It was weak, fading, chronically aching.

Eugene lifted his pristine leather shoe and pounded the heel down upon the side of Gus's head.

A chug of water cascaded internally, and Gus was sure that it was blood dripping down his ear canal.

Eugene went to strike again, but something caught his attention.

It took a few seconds longer for Gus to register it, but he heard it too.

An explosion.

On the ground floor.

And the sound of gushing water.

Yes, Whizzo. Yes, Desert.

They'd done it.

"Looks like your army won't be invading anywhere after all."

Eugene's arrogance faded and his wrath took over, prompting him to pack even more strength behind his next punch.

Chapter Fifty

It was too late to get to the corridor.

Whizzo's invention was just too great.

Even if they did get to the door, if they opened it the water would be released and the army would escape.

In the end, Whizzo and Desert had no choice but to embrace the flood.

The army sprinted toward Whizzo but didn't get to him. Their arms stretched and their fingers scraped his jaw but the water took them in its arms and lifted them up, throwing them chaotically to and fro.

Whizzo swam toward Desert and grabbed her hand.

The water level was rising so rapidly there was no time for them to talk. No pause for breath or break for talking. They had no chance to form a plan – they just had to allow themselves to be lifted upwards.

At least they could keep their heads above water. To look down was to witness the greatest massacre of the infected since London.

The bodies of the army squirmed, arms reached out, eyes

widened. A few were already limp and the rest were getting there.

The plan had worked.

Damn, it had worked.

But how were they going to get out?

The ceiling was approaching as the water level rose. Whizzo estimated less than a minute until the entire room was full and there would be no place for air.

Whizzo finally gained enough thought to turn to Desert, who was looking back at him with fear and resignation in her eyes.

"What do we do?" Whizzo cried, his voice drowned by gushing water.

"What?" Desert shouted, unable to hear him above the rising tide.

"I said, what do we do?"

Desert looked around.

What could they do?

Were they even meant to survive?

Maybe this was it. Save the world and die doing so. Become a martyr that would never be forgotten because they were never remembered in the first place.

"I love you," Whizzo said. "You're my best friend."

"Don't do that," Desert said.

"Do what?"

"You know. Don't act like we aren't going to get out of this."

Whizzo looked around and shrugged, desperately paddling to keep afloat, rising with the surface, approaching the ceiling with imminent doom.

"I think it's probably time to accept we're out of luck," Whizzo said.

Desert looked around. She pointed at something.

"There!"

Whizzo peered to where she was pointing. A shaft. A small one, mind, probably not big enough for them to fit.

"I don't know if–"

His sentence was muffled by the water and they submitted to being under. The room was now a large box of ocean, and they could do nothing but look at each other and hold their breath.

Whizzo saw his final few air bubbles creep away.

Desert beckoned Whizzo and began her swim toward the shaft. Whizzo reluctantly followed. He wasn't optimistic, but he also wasn't about to die without her next to him.

It took longer than he thought it would. His arms were aching, his body growing weary as he was deprived of oxygen.

They reached the shaft and Desert tried to fit.

She couldn't.

She waved for him to go through and he refused.

Her face curled into annoyance and she pushed him into the shaft.

Reluctantly, he climbed through, feeling the walls enclose around him, claustrophobia never more apparent.

He looked back at Desert, who waved for him to go, and tried to get in.

Whizzo twitched. A minor convulsion as he grew dizzy.

He pulled himself further through the shaft, and further still, finding his body working slower and slower.

The shaft directed him vertically. He pulled himself upwards and finally found his way to the water's surface.

He lifted his head above the water and took a large intake of breath.

As his mind returned and the patches left his vision, he looked up to see light.

There was a way out.

He turned to tell Desert.

She wasn't there.

Desert was not there.

He looked back to the light, then back to the water.

He took a few more breaths, then took a large one and plunged himself back under.

He travelled through the shaft and returned to Desert's body.

It was limp.

He could not tell if she was dead or unconscious.

He did not care.

He grabbed hold of her arm and pulled her into the shaft.

She wouldn't fit.

He swam behind her, straightened her body and pushed her instead.

Chapter Fifty-One

Where was that damn gun?

Gus knew he'd brought one.

But he'd thrown it away.

He'd shown it to Donny and thrown it away to show that he was ready to be killed, that he wasn't going to hurt Donny, that he was prepared to be unarmed.

Now he really needed it.

Eugene grabbed Gus by the throat and hoisted him into the air, pushing him against the wall. Gus battered his fists against Eugene's arms, but it was like a kitten fighting a lion.

Gus used to be the lion and Eugene used to be the kitten – but the greatest trick the lion ever played was convincing the lion tamer that it was working.

Gus choked, but didn't give up yet, as he watched Sadie rise from her huddle and dive upon Eugene's back. Eugene refused to let Gus's throat go at first, but once she had bitten into his neck, he had no choice but to release him.

Gus dropped, landing on his elbow, sure that he heard it crack.

And then he saw it.

Around the corner of the corridor.

Glinting in the reflection of the artificial light.

He was distracted by the wild screams of Sadie's terror as she was grabbed from Eugene's back and thrown across the corridor. She landed on her back and took to her feet.

Gus went to run, but Eugene stomped a foot on the back of his one real leg, making Gus kneel and scream.

"Wherever did you get this leg from?" Eugene asked, looking at Gus's artificial limb.

Gus ignored the question and went to punch the knee of Eugene's leg that pressed down upon his calf. Eugene batted it away like he was swatting a fly.

Eugene did scream, however, from the unexpected bite of Sadie's sharp teeth in the back of his leg.

This gave Gus the second he needed to free himself and continue his run.

Eugene plunged his fist downwards and into Sadie's head.

The poor thing wasn't used to taking a beating. Gus had taken many and was used to battling through pain – but he was sure that Sadie hadn't lost a battle in her short life. He winced as she yelped, falling into a pool of her own blood.

He wanted to go back and help her, to make sure she was okay, but their only chance was for him to retrieve his gun.

He made it to within an arm's reach, but Eugene grabbed him by the back of the neck. Gus swung his boot between Eugene's legs and Eugene instinctively loosened his grip for a moment.

Finally, Gus had the opportunity to grab the gun.

Eugene can't have realised, as he went to punch Gus again, successfully meeting a bloody nose with his bloody fist.

"You're untrained," Gus muttered.

"What?" Eugene snarled.

Gus rolled onto his back, onto the hand holding the gun.

"You think you can beat the shit out of me. Yeah, fine. But you've got the ability and none of the awareness."

"Awareness! You are–"

Gus revealed the gun and pointed it upwards at Eugene.

Sadie, who was just about to pounce, paused.

Eugene, who was just about to strike, hesitated.

"That's the thing, isn't it?" Gus mused. He went to give a cocky smile, but it hurt too much to move his cheeks.

"What?" Eugene retorted, venomous and hostile.

"Nature versus nurture and all that."

"I don't know what you are talking about, but–"

"Basically, you can pump yourself full of nature's toxin – but you're still a weak little prick."

Eugene went to retort but was cut off by a gunshot, and the bullet that found its way through his open mouth and out the top of his skull.

Chapter Fifty-Two

❦

Whizzo pushed with all he had.

She was practically stuck in the shaft now, but that was fine, as every time he pushed her, she shifted a little further.

But pushing under the water was tough.

And the water was stinging the open wound of his missing finger.

He needed to pant. To breathe. To gather strength and allow oxygen to his muscles. He was using oxygen at a greater rate and he knew he was in danger of passing out himself.

But he would not give up.

Desert would not have given up for him.

So he pushed.

And pushed and pushed.

And twitched.

He felt his body shutting down. No longer responding to him. A disobedient dog turning on its owner. A drunk rebelling against their poison.

He went to take a breath and remembered he couldn't. He

choked on water then came to terms with it being there and allowed it to settle into his lungs.

A body floated past his face, making him jump. The open eyes of the genetically superior infected stared as the empty corpse travelled onwards.

He entered the shaft himself, using his shoulder to push Desert further.

She shifted ever so slightly.

He had to get out himself now. But that was no longer possible – she was blocking his escape.

So he had to push.

For both their sakes.

His eyelids drooped; his body emptied itself of tension.

He was slipping away, and he knew it.

He convulsed; this time harder.

With a surge of energy, he pushed as hard as he could against the water and rammed his head into Desert's backside. Using the walls of the shaft he forced her forward.

He fell limp.

And he reminded himself he couldn't.

He couldn't give in to fatality.

He couldn't give up his consciousness.

Because that's how it would start – with his unconsciousness. Like Desert. Then he would gradually settle into an eager death.

He pushed her once more.

Nearly there.

Nearly...

What?

Nearly what?

His thoughts were leaving him.

He gave a final push and she reached the vertical part of the shaft. Her body floated upwards and Whizzo watched her go, watched her as she rose to the surface, rose to the air.

Watched her as he fell behind.

His body wouldn't move any longer.

He was so tired. His body felt so light.

Is this what dying felt like?

And, with that final thought, he passed out.

Chapter Fifty-Three

A vague sense of satisfaction filled Gus's poisonous mind as he watched Eugene Squire's body thud to the ground.

He always expected to feel bad for causing death, but he often didn't.

It was always the enemy who died.

He fought the Taliban in Afghanistan and never once hesitated in firing his gun – and he didn't hesitate this time either.

Eugene deserved death.

Then again, death was the easy way out – he deserved a far graver consequence. But who would put him in prison?

Did prisons even exist anymore?

Gus thought of how Eugene would have been treated in prison and it gave him a distant smile; a smile that faded as soon as he remembered why he was there.

He daren't look at Donny yet.

He wasn't ready.

Instead, he looked at Sadie, who was on her knees, staring at him with that same vulnerable look his daughter used to give him when she was scared or being told off.

He was never that good at telling her off. She made him too soft. She was the only one who could warm his frozen heart and she must have known it, because she pulled those eyes every time he attempted to be a disciplinarian.

And here they were again, in Sadie's eyes.

Sadie looked over Gus's shoulder.

He knew what she was looking at, but he didn't want to look at it, so he kept looking at her.

Once he looked at it, it was real.

Once he saw it, he would have witnessed incontrovertible proof.

Once he saw it, Donny would be dead.

For now, Donny was still alive in his thoughts. Waiting to be rescued. Waiting to pummel Gus to within an inch of his life and be saved, because that was what the plan was, and it was working – damn, it was working.

And now...

Sadie bowed her head. She sobbed. Quietly and ashamedly.

"It's okay," Gus told her.

Those eyes looked up at him again.

"It's okay to cry," he said, despite never having believed such a statement himself. He cried when his family died, but never before and never since. It was a weakness he would not allow himself.

"It is, honestly," he insisted. "It's okay to..."

He dropped his head and closed his eyes so he didn't cry himself.

It wasn't a weakness.

Donny had taught him that – had taught him that suppressing emotions isn't what makes you a man.

He turned his head slightly, and he could see the body out of the corner of his eye, so he turned his head back.

He was going to have to look.

Get it over with, he begged himself.

Come on, he cajoled.

Just do it.

He stood. Wiped the profusely bleeding features of his face on a sleeve that was already crusted with dried blood.

And he turned.

And he saw it.

Not moving. Not twitching. Not thinking or talking or fighting or doing anything that someone alive would do.

He walked over, stumbling from wall to wall, and fell to his knees beside Donny's head.

He tried lifting the head and shaking it, but it was heavy in the way that only a corpse was.

"Go find the others," Gus told Sadie.

Sadie shook her head, adamant that she would not leave.

"Do it," Gus insisted. "There's nothing else we can do here, find them and make sure they are okay."

With a reluctant stutter, she ran.

He was left alone.

Just him and his buddy.

Just them and the lie he'd just told.

There's nothing else we can do here.

The water was leaking through the walls.

The compound was about to be destroyed, and all the knowledge within it.

But the facility still remained.

And Gus had a decision to make.

Within the facility's walls was the research that would potentially cure the infection. The knowledge and substances created that someone with a far greater mind could utilise to create a cure, or at least a vaccine.

The end of the world could be over.

But then again, inside those walls was the research to create a vastly superior army that a deluded dictator could use to cause further genocide. The knowledge and substances created within those walls could mean that someone with a far greater mind could cause the death and suffering of those that still remained alive.

The question for Gus was how much he trusted the human race.

How much he trusted others finding this information and how they would use it.

In the end, he didn't even need to think about it.

He knew what he thought of the human race.

And he knew what he had to do.

Chapter Fifty-Four

Sadie found Desert's unconscious body laying atop damp grass. The opening to a vent beside her was pouring with water, drenching her body.

Sadie grabbed hold of Desert's leg and dragged her, pulling her away from the cascading water leaking from the side of the compound. The whole place looked to be filled, and there were no longer any crevasses that were not leaking.

She lay Desert's body beneath the shadow of a tree, using stray leaves as a cushion, and waited.

Desert's eyes didn't open.

Sadie pushed her, prodded her, pulled on her arm – but Desert didn't respond.

"Nnnmm," Sadie moaned.

Why wasn't she waking up?

She placed an ear beside Desert's mouth and felt no breath against her cheek.

And she recalled what she had to do.

She lifted her hands in the air, balled them together into a combined fist, and brought them hurtling down upon Desert's chest. She waited a moment, then did the same again. And again. And again.

What else had Desert shown her?

She pinched Desert's nose and opened her mouth. She breathed into it, long breaths, long and hard, just as she remembered.

She waited a moment.

Then did the same. Pinched nose, open mouth, long hard breaths.

Pinched nose.

Open mouth.

Long, hard breaths.

Fists combined, strike upon chest, again, and again.

Pinched nose.

Open mouth.

Long, hard breaths.

Why wasn't she waking up?

Desert had said that's when someone would wake up.

She brought her fists down upon Desert's chest once more, and a spluttering of water fell out of her mouth and dribbled down her chin.

She repeated the action and water dribbled out once again.

She repeated it, and only a little water fell out.

Desert choked.

She choked!

Sadie brought her fists down again and Desert choked up another gurgle of water.

Pinched nose.

Open mouth.

Long, hard breaths.

And another. And another.

Desert coughed.

This was it!

Pinched.

Open.

Breath.

Pinched.

Open.

Breath.

Pinched.

Open.

Br–

Desert's eyes opened. She sucked in a large intake of air.

Sadie stumbled backwards, grinning with excitement, delirious with palpable giddiness.

Desert kept breathing in large wheezes of air, again and again, and again, and again.

Sadie returned to Desert's side, and looked her in the eyes, deeply and contently.

She'd done it.

"You..." Desert mumbled, failing in her words, then trying again. "You did... You did CPR... On me..."

Sadie nodded eagerly.

Desert lifted a weary hand and placed it on Sadie's cheek.

"Well done you," Desert said.

Sadie beamed, as proud as she could ever be.

"Where's Whizzo?" Desert asked, looking around.

Sadie looked up.

Where was Whizzo?

"Where is he?" Desert repeated, leaning up then falling back down with exhaustion.

Sadie stood. Looked to one side of her, to the other. Sniffed. Listened.

And looked back at the leaking vent.

Then back at Desert.

"Where is Whizzo!" Desert cried, more hysteria and urgency to her voice – at least, as much as her weakened body would allow.

But she already had her answer.

"No..."

She fell back to the surface.

Sadie went to her side and stroked the hair from Desert's face. It was drenched.

"We..." Sadie tried.

"What?"

"We..." Sadie tried again. "We... won."

"We what?"

"We won," Sadie said, this time with more confidence.

Desert looked back at the building.

They had won.

Whizzo was a genius.

And now he was gone.

Yet she was alive, and the last thing she remembered was being underwater and watching Whizzo disappear through that ventilation shaft.

The one now flooded and overflowing.

"Whizzo..." she whispered. "You idiot."

Chapter Fifty-Five

The crumbling walls of the darkened facility were home to nothing but the roaming, content dead. They were dormant, hovering mindlessly, as at peace as the undead could be.

It was quiet. Nothing but the occasional groan or grunt at what was perceived to be a disturbance but was barely even a sound.

Nothing could disturb the silence.

Except that wasn't exactly true.

A bloodied face upon a scarred and wounded body stared through the dirty windscreen of a jeep – a jeep that had been swiftly stolen from some recently deceased guards outside the compound.

Gus Harvey paused the jeep outside the facility, looking upon the broken faces of the infected aimlessly wandering the perimeter.

There was knowledge left strewn across the floor of this facility that could either prove a gift to the human race, or an outlet for the most evil urges of the human condition.

Gus was not taking any chances.

He stepped out of the jeep and dragged himself across the side of it, holding up his body that was losing energy faster than he was losing patience.

He took out a knife and swung it into the side of the petrol tank. Petrol instantly began to spray the ground beneath, and so he hurried back to the driver's seat and began steering.

He directed the car toward the building and drove around the wall's edge.

The disturbance attracted the infected and what had previously been sparsely placed absent zombies was now a sickening horde, charging toward him.

He sped up.

Not that he cared all that much for his own precious life – but the job needed to be done before he could meet his demise; if he was, in fact, going to meet his demise in these moments.

Once he had made his way around the entire building, he drove out to the perimeter, to the broken fences, and sped around them. He noticed the petrol growing less in quantity, until it was just intermittent sprays. He finished his second circle of the facility, the jeep chugging and jolting, and he knew he was almost done.

A glance in the mirror showed many hungry infected still following him around.

The jeep came to a halt and would not move any longer. He climbed out of the smashed window and pulled himself atop the roof.

There they all stood. Rocking the jeep, reaching for him as he struggled to keep his balance. His fading awareness and intensifying pain didn't make such a task any easier – but he could see the infected covering themselves in unleaded as they clambered for him. Some of them slipped and knocked others over and this prompted a snort of ironic laughter from Gus.

A year of fearing these things just to discover that they weren't the scariest things that existed.

He took out his lighter.

"I'm sorry, Donny," he said, knowing that the dead didn't listen. "I promise I won't let anyone else ever be like you again."

He threw the lighter upon the horde of zombies and leapt from the jeep to a nearby bush.

They were up in flames before Gus's foot had landed amongst the twigs.

He backed away just in time to see the jeep explode.

He backed away further and watched as the infected fell, struggling under the weight of the fire.

And then the fire spread. Across the path he had driven the jeep, to the walls of the facility.

And there went the facility, and everything in it.

The place that had been his prison for months.

Where they had tortured Sadie. Changed Donny. Removed his leg.

The accumulated knowledge to change the world.

The walls collapsed, the interior destroyed, and a huge cloud of smoke covered the air above, masking the sun in thick puffs of pollution.

Gus stayed to watch a little longer.

To get that little bit of satisfaction, that slight reprieve. To witness what he did in Donny's memory.

To witness the death sentence for the world's salvation, whilst witnessing the beginning of hope for the new world's state of being.

Goodbye Eugene Squire.

Goodbye the facility.

Goodbye Donny Jevon.

BEFORE

Chapter Fifty-Six

Something awoke Gus, and it took a few seconds of grogginess to realise what it was. He lifted his arm from its place around his sleeping wife and looked to the younger face peering up at him from the end of the bed.

"Daddy!" cried Laney.

Gus gently shushed her.

"Don't wake Mum," he told her, then waved her closer. She ran to his side. "What is it?"

"I had a bad dream."

"Oh no. What happened?"

"I – I don't want to say."

"Well you know it was just a dream, don't you?"

"But it felt real."

"Dreams often do. Come on, let's get you back to bed."

He hoisted her up and carried her, glancing at the alarm clock. It was gone three in the morning.

He placed her back into her bed and pulled the covers over her.

"Would you like me to check your room?" he asked. He'd often done this after nightmares – checking the room for monsters of her subconscious just to prove that they weren't really there.

She shook her head.

Strange, she always wanted him to check her room after a nightmare.

"Are you sure?" he asked.

She nodded.

"My dream wasn't about monsters in my room," she told him. "It was about you."

He nodded. This made sense. He'd returned from his third tour of Afghanistan a few weeks ago, and Janet had told him how difficult it had been for her – especially during the most recent tour. She was now old enough that she could start to understand where he was and what he was doing. There were conversations at school and things she'd hear on the news, and she was bound to begin to link it all together.

"Oh," Gus said. "Well I'm back now. Nothing bad's going to happen to me."

With the bullet lodged in his calf meaning he wouldn't be returning to Afghanistan any time soon, he could actually say this with some sincerity.

"It wasn't about you going away," she told him, her voice small.

"It wasn't?"

"It was about you being hurt here."

"Here? In London?"

She nodded.

"Laney, the Taliban aren't going to come to London."

"No, it wasn't... It wasn't them..."

Gus grew confused.

"Well nothing's going to happen to me here," he told her.

"You don't know that."

"Yes, I do."

She shook her head. So adamant, so stubborn. Just like her mother.

"What would happen to me here?" he asked.

"In my dream you were all alone... Me and Mummy weren't there... It was just you..."

"Just me?"

"I don't know where we were, but there were bad people, and they were trying to get you."

"Bad people?"

"Yes, with horrible eyes and limps and all covered in blood and stuff."

Covered in blood?

What kind of shows had she been watching? Where on earth had that come from?

He took a deep breath, held it, and let it go.

"I don't know what it is you saw, but it was just a nightmare."

"But it felt so real."

"Well, it wasn't."

He pulled the duvet up and tucked her in, tightening it across her in the way that always made him feel so secure when he was a child – those rare times his mum was sober enough to do it.

"Promise me something, Dad."

"What would you like me to promise you?"

"That whatever happens to me and mum, you will still be okay."

"Whatever would happen to–"

"Promise it, Daddy. Please!"

He hesitated.

"I promise."

"I love you, Dad."

"I love you too, Laney. Now go to sleep."

She nodded. He kissed her forehead, stood, and watched her fall back to what he hoped was a more peaceful slumber.

And, just as he went to leave the room, he paused in the doorway. Looked back at her sleeping face.

It was a strange nightmare for a child to have.

A strange request for a child to make.

But she was a smart kid. Her brain worked a million miles per hour, far quicker than any other child.

Maybe she was too smart.

No, she could never be too smart.

She was perfect.

"Sweet dreams," Gus whispered, and closed the door behind him.

AFTER THE END

Chapter Fifty-Seven

The rain seemed to be never-ending. Its incessant downpour had begun the moment the opposition fell and continued for months afterwards.

It was fitting, therefore, that the first day that the rain ceased and the sun announced itself, that Gus found himself able to step outside.

It had taken a long time to heal. In fact, from the state he had been in, he wasn't exactly clear how he'd been walking around or, indeed, alive.

He woke up one afternoon, water pounding the weak window of a room he did not recognise. Sadie was asleep in the corner. He assumed he had been unconscious for a day.

But once Desert came in and spoke to him, he'd learnt that it had been more like months.

She regrettably admitted she gave up at one point. That, without any machines or way of knowing if Gus was in fact braindead, it was becoming pointless just sitting around waiting for him to wake up. His broken rib, broken nose and shattered cheek bones had mended themselves, but Gus's feeble, battered mind seemed to be struggling.

Desert had said that the only reason they didn't give up was because of Sadie. Apparently, when Desert tried to drag her away, Sadie had completely refused to leave Gus's side.

This made him smile. That girl could barely talk to him, yet she was faithful to the last, and far cleverer than she appeared.

Desert had looted a nearby hospital and barely made it out alive, saved by Sadie at least twice. They had returned to find Gus still unmoved, but with enough supplies to sustain him for another few weeks.

And now, using his leg for the first time in a while and leaning against a crutch, he looked down to where his artificial limb used to be. Desert said it had jammed itself further in and they'd had to remove it for risk of infection.

Gus had shrugged and nodded. He was alive, and to them he was grateful – but he had no idea, nor could he begin to understand, how exactly he was still alive.

He stood atop a verge that allowed him to look over a view of fields and houses as far as he could see. The kind of view he'd once described as breath-taking. In the distance he could see a blackened building; the facility, or what remained of it.

"You all right?" came a voice behind him.

He turned and looked at her.

"I'm good," he said. "But I was thinking."

"What's that?"

"The fight is done. How about we drop the name now. I mean, Desert – I never really liked it."

She laughed.

"Fine." She stepped forward and offered a hand. "The name is Lucy Sanders. Nice to meet you."

He stretched an arm from his crutch and took her hand. He held it rather than shook it, and smiled at her.

"Thank you," he told her.

She nodded.

Sadie appeared over her shoulder.

Sweet, sweet Sadie. A girl he had originally only kept with him because she could fight, and because she could hold the key to defeating the infection.

Funny, really – how all of those things seemed so unimportant now.

"Tea's ready," Lucy said. "Sadie caught a rabbit and she's quite proud of it. I think she wants you to come and taste it."

Sadie nodded eagerly.

"I'll be there in a moment."

"Want any help coming in?"

"I'll be fine."

Lucy nodded and returned to the broken-down house they had made their home for the past few months.

Sadie remained. Waiting for him, looking worried, as if she thought Gus was about to do something bad.

"I'll be in in a moment," Gus told her. When she looked wounded, he added, "I promise."

She smiled and returned inside.

Gus looked back to the view.

He'd burnt the facility. But there was still one more thing to let go of.

He took it out of his pocket. Thumbed through the pages. Looked over the cover. Choked on the dust that rose off it.

The Ever-present.

An awful book, really.

But one that meant a lot.

He took his lighter and produced the flame, attaching the spark to the corner.

He threw it into the view and watched it fall down the hill, burning, ending, and ceasing to be, until the fire was gone and the book was a blackened mess, just like the facility.

That blackened mess fell down the hill, ashes marking its path.

He kept his eyes on the book for one second longer – just long enough to whisper something.

Then he returned inside, the words he'd whispered hanging on the brief sunshine and turning to ash themselves.

"I promise, Laney."

ALSO BY RICK WOOD

After the Devil Has Won - a post apocalyptic thriller

The Sensitives - a paranormal horror series

Plus many more, all available to look through at www. rickwoodwriter.com/books

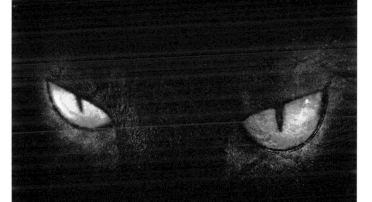

CIA ROSE BOOK ONE

AFTER THE DEVIL HAS WON

RICK WOOD

RICK WOOD

THE SENSITIVES

BOOK ONE

20103439R00166

Printed in Great Britain
by Amazon